It has been said that there is a book in everyone. Well, during lockdown 2021, Robert decided it was his time. He had this idea and put pen to paper and after 18 months, he would like to present it to you. Robert is 67 with a wife of 27 years, three grown up children and eleven grandchildren that keep him busy all the time. He lives in Huddersfield, in the Pennines and loves it there. He hopes you love the book, especially the devastating end.

I would like to dedicate the book to my wife Julie, my granddaughter Rachel and my sister Susan, who put up with me over the eighteen months; they lifted me up when I had writer's block and cheered me on when it was going well.

Robert D Shaw

WHERE IS AMANDA?

Is She Ever Going to Be Found

AUSTIN MACAULEY PUBLISHERS™

LONDON • CAMBRIDGE • NEW YORK • SHARJAH

A CIP catalogue record for this title is available from the British Library.

ISBN 9781035865062 (Paperback)
ISBN 9781035865079 (Hardback)
ISBN 9781035865086 (ePub e-book)

www.austinmacauley.com

First Published 2024
Austin Macauley Publishers Ltd®
1 Canada Square
Canary Wharf
London
E14 5AA

Firstly, I acknowledge Adam Shaw and Michael Cowan, who read the book on numerous occasions and gave me their honest opinions, which I liked most of the time but not all the time. Secondly, to all my family and friends who had to put up with me going on about my book. I'm sure they got sick of it. Sorry.

Chapter 1

Aaron stood over his wife, laughing. It had been a good night out, their monthly date night. His wife, Beth, had just fallen off the bed, laughing. They had always liked to experiment and on this occasion, it had got a bit out of hand.

"What the hell were you thinking?" said Beth.

"It was good while it lasted." Aaron smiled.

"Sometimes, I wonder what goes through that mind of yours," Beth replied, trying to get up.

"Here, let me help you up. Hold on this time."

Aaron got hold of her hands and gently pulled her up. Aaron leaned in to kiss her when Amanda rushed in.

"What's all the noise?" concerned and wondering what the noise was all about. She quickly turned around with a cry. "Disgusting!"

At the sight of their daughter, looking horrified, Aaron and Beth landed on the bed in fits of laughter.

"Maybe we shouldn't have had that last bottle of wine," Beth said.

Aaron put on his dressing gown and walked to the door.

"I'll see how she is, can't be good. I remember walking in on my parents, I had nightmares for a week."

Amanda sat on the bed, texting someone, probably her best friend Maggie. Aaron sat gently next to her. He hoped the message wasn't about what had just happened.

"Sorry about that," Aaron said. "We were just fooling around, having a bit of fun."

Amanda looked up from her phone and gave him a look that would have made the ground swallow him up.

"Oh, come on, Amanda, I'm sure you and Matt have your moments," he said with a smile. Amanda just got up and stared back.

"Dad, it's nothing to do with you, and stay out of my business."

Aaron looked a bit hurt. "I'll see you in the morning, and we can talk about this if you want to." He turned to walk out.

"At least we do it in an empty house," retorted Amanda.

He thought, *so much for keeping out of her business.*

Beth was just getting into bed when he got back, all thoughts of romance gone out of the window.

"How did it go?" she asked.

He sat down and looked at her. "She thinks we are disgusting. I just said we were having a bit of fun. I did say, I'm sure you and Matt have your moments."

Beth laughed. "I bet that went down well."

Aaron nodded. "Oh yes, I was told to mind my own business and it was nothing to do with me."

He took his dressing gown off and slipped into bed, Beth putting her arm around his waist, saying, "Oh, the joy of being parents."

***

Amanda was already up when Beth went into the kitchen and got a look that could kill.

"Morning," said Beth, as happily as she could, hoping it would cool things down. "What have you got planned for today? Are you seeing Matt today? Your dad and I thought we'd go out for Sunday lunch, if you're interested? Bring Matt along. It would be nice for all of us to get together."

Luke, Amanda's brother, stood at the door, listening and deciding what to say, he didn't think anyone had seen him. Luke was like that, he seemed to float around like a ghost. You never knew where he was.

Luke was twelve and quite a character. He had blonde hair too, well, mousey blond and it fell to his shoulders. He never kept it clean and it was always all over the place. He was just starting to get teenager spots on his face, he said it didn't bother him, though it would later in life.

Luke had a 'nothing bothered him' attitude, which was great most of the time but when it came to big problems, it stank. His favourite saying was 'Whatever'.

"I'm not going anywhere if Matt's coming," Luke said in a grumpy voice and it sounded like he meant it.

Amanda swung around and gave the same look she'd delivered Beth when she had walked in. It seemed Luke was going to get killed by the stare as well.

"Don't be like that, Luke," Beth said, "you and Matt normally get along, don't you?"

Amanda flung her arms in the air. "This little shit is accusing Matt of breaking the controller for his bloody Xbox, Mum."

Luke glared at her. "He did!"

"It was an accident, Luke. If you hadn't left it on your bedroom floor, Matt wouldn't have stepped on it, and what was it doing on the bloody floor anyway?" Amanda shouted.

"It's my bedroom, I'll put things where I want; and what was he doing in my bedroom in the first place?" Luke said angrily.

Amanda was now going red with rage. Beth knew she would have to break in at any moment.

"Right, stop this now!" Beth shouted. "Luke, you are coming with us this lunch time and we'll sort this controller out another time. I'm not having that sort of language in this house. Amanda, you've been brought up better than that."

It went quiet for a moment. Amanda got up. "I'm going to Matt's. I might see you later."

Luke turned and stomped off to his bedroom, barging past Aaron on the way out. "Whoa! What was all that noise? What happened?" Aaron looked at Beth.

"Don't worry, it's just a normal Sunday morning, darling."

***

Aaron was a programmer for IBM and did troubleshooting for IBM's corporate clients. He loved his job and most of his work could be done from home, but sometimes, he would have to travel at a moment's notice, anywhere in the world. This had not been a problem when he started as a junior technician but as he got more involved and became more adept at programming, his life got more complicated. Long meetings, coming home late at night and the trips abroad had made for a corrosive atmosphere at home.

Aaron and Beth loved each other, though over the years it had turned from being in love with each other, to loving the idea. They both had secrets, which were never brought up, it had been a cancer in their relationship. Like any marriage, there were ups and downs, but recently, it seemed that they were trying hard to get on a bit better. Hence, the idea of the date nights, which were working well.

In the past, they had tried to keep it away from Amanda and Luke, although it wasn't working. When Aaron was away abroad, Amanda didn't look forward to his homecoming and made any excuse not be there. Amanda had heard the arguments, the bickering. To her, it was like a competition of 'he said, she said' but no one was winning.

Amanda loved her parents when they were happy, even though she had intentionally walked in on them last night. Yes, it was disgusting and maybe she shouldn't have done it, but she worried about her mum. What was Dad doing to her mum?

Imagination is a strange bedfellow and Amanda's went into overdrive hearing the noises. Amanda had tried to bring things up in a conversation with her mum previously and Mum always laughed it off, telling her not to be so stupid as everything was alright. Amanda wasn't too sure.

Chapter 2

Aaron and Beth were walking through the carpark of the Foundry Inn in Poole. They lived in Poole, about two miles away. They had been living there for about ten years after moving from Basingstoke.

"Come on, Luke! The tables booked for one o'clock, we're going to be late," Beth said in a get-here-now voice.

Luke gave that look back that said "whatever?" Aaron and Beth were talking when Luke ran ahead and into the doorway of the Foundry Inn. Aaron found Luke telling the receptionist that he had a table booked under the name of Simpson for five.

"Thank you for doing that," Aaron said, "does that mean you're going to pay the bill?"

Luke, looking up, said quietly, "No."

The receptionist picked five menu cards up and asked them to follow her. Aaron told the girl that there would be two more joining them soon. Luke sat at the table first, with Beth and Aaron choosing to sit opposite each other. Beth looked distracted and in her own little world.

"What's wrong, Mum?" Luke asked.

Beth looked at Luke, knowing he'd said something but it hadn't registered.

"Beth, you alright?" Aaron was looking concerned.

"What?" Beth looked at them both.

"Are you alright, you look miles away?" replied Aaron.

Beth sighed, "Oh, I was just thinking of what happened this morning, maybe I was a bit harsh on Amanda."

Beth had always been protective of Amanda, she hadn't had the best time of her sixteen years on this earth. When she was born, she was perfect, Aaron and Beth were so excited to take her home and show her off to the family.

Beth was eighteen and Aaron was twenty when Amanda arrived. They knew they were young and were set on not being like all the other young parents, being determined to raise Amanda in a loving and safe environment. They had got married the year before, after they found out that Beth was three months pregnant, Aaron thinking it was the right thing to do and he loved Beth to bits. She was only seventeen but Aaron just took it in his stride.

When Amanda was eight, she started sleeping a lot, not eating, and when Beth managed to get some food down her, it came back up an hour later. She was always complaining of headaches and having little tantrums, which wasn't like her. This had been going on for about a week.

Aaron thought it was only a tummy bug, but Beth thought it was time to go to the doctor's. Beth explained the symptoms to the receptionist over the phone and it was agreed that Beth should bring Amanda down that morning.

Aaron was at work; he'd been called to a meeting in Basingstoke. She tried to reach him, but his mobile was turned off, leaving a message and texting him, explaining what was happening. Beth hoped that he would be out of his meeting soon.

Beth arrived at the surgery and had to wait about an hour before being called in, the receptionist kept apologising. She too was concerned, as the surgery was busy and Amanda was playing up. The family doctor was Dr Hameed, he was great.

When anything needed looking at, he was there, especially when it came to children. The receptionist called them over and said Dr Hameed was ready for them, room three. Beth picked Amanda up and walked her in. Dr Hameed looked up from his desk.

"Well hello, you two. How are you both, and which one's the patient, now?" He saw straight away the problem was with Amanda. "Oh, I see, what's been happening?"

As Beth went through everything, he tried to take Amanda's temperature and blood pressure, with great difficulty, but managed in the end. He looked in her ears and then her eyes, stating as he looked up, "I think we'll send her up to A&E, just as a precaution. How long did you say she'd been like this?"

Beth replied, "Oh, about a week, ten days. We thought she was just playing up. What do you think it is, Dr Hameed?"

Dr Hameed looked a bit sheepish. "There seems to be a little problem with Amanda's eyes. It's best to check it out, better to be safe, than sorry."

Beth looked worried. "Is it serious?"

"Let them have a look and we'll take it from there."

14

"Which hospital, Poole or Bournemouth?" Beth asked.

Dr Hameed confirmed Bournemouth. This made Beth even more anxious and she could have done with Aaron being there. Bournemouth was the regional hospital and was there for major problems. Dr Hameed checked if she could get to the hospital and that Beth was okay driving.

"I'll ring A&E and tell them to expect you," said Dr Hammed.

Beth looked at Dr Hammed again, her eyes watering.

"Everything is going to be alright, Beth, let's see what the doctors say at the hospital."

Everything was going through Beth's mind as she drove to Bournemouth, from the surgery it would take about thirty minutes, but it felt like hours, *what the hell was wrong,* Beth thought.

She arrived at A&E to find that Amanda didn't want to go in. Beth tried to persuade her but Amanda was not having any of it. Beth was trying to explain why it was important, nothing was going to happen to her and that Mummy would be there all the time.

Her phone rang. Beth couldn't find her phone in her bag, where was it? Thinking, why she put all this crap in here, she just emptied the contents on the passenger seat and there it was, ringing and vibrating at her. It was Aaron.

"Sorry, I couldn't have my phone switched on. Saw you'd called. How did it go at the doctor's?" He asked.

Beth started tearing up. Aaron was now concerned.

"What is it love, where are you? I didn't get all that you said on your message."

Beth tried to calm down and tell him what had happened at the doctor's. "I'm outside Bournemouth A&E but Amanda is scared, and she won't go in." Help, I need you.

Aaron asked to speak to her and Beth gave the phone to Amanda.

"It's Daddy," said Aaron.

"Hello, Daddy," she said.

He could hear the fear in her voice. "Are you alright, darling?"

Amanda started to cry and if he could, he would have given her the most amazing hug. Amanda pushed the phone back to Mummy, still crying. Aaron heard Beth on the phone.

"Give the phone back to Amanda, please?" Amanda was calming down a bit. "Amanda darling, I have finished my meeting at work and I am on my way, can you promise me that you'll go with Mummy to see the doctor? You know doctors make you feel better, but they have to find out what's wrong, don't they?"

Amanda didn't reply.

"Don't you think the doctors need to see you, to find out what's wrong and make you better?" Saying it again, but softer.

Amanda thought a bit and said in a little quiet voice, "Yes, Daddy."

Aaron was relieved. "Okay, look Amanda, it won't be long before I'm there next to you giving you big Daddy hugs, and when it's all over, I'll take you and Mummy for a McDonald's, how does that sound?"

Amanda seemed to pick up a bit. "Can I have chicken nuggets and fries?"

"Yes of course, I know they're your favourite."

"Can I have a strawberry milkshake as well, Daddy?"

Beth came on the phone. "It's amazing how a bit of bribery works."

Aaron replied with a chuckle, "If it gets her to see the doctor, I'm in. Look, I'm on my way, just got to finish up here, shouldn't take me more than fifteen to twenty minutes and I'll be on the M3. I should be there in a couple of hours. Look, I know this is easy to say, but keep calm and don't show Amanda you're worried. It's like Dr Hammed said, it's all going to be alright."

There was a long pause before he got an answer.

"Dr Hammed wouldn't have suggested we went to hospital if there wasn't something wrong, Aaron."

He knew she was right.

"Beth, I love you, I'll be there as soon as I can."

***

Aaron looked up from his menu. "Have you decided what you want? I'm having the roast beef dinner, what about you, Beth?"

"Do you know, I might have the steak and ale pie this time, I ordered it a month ago, and it was lovely."

Aaron turned to Luke, giving him suggestions, but nothing floated his boat. "Come on, Luke, we haven't got all day, make a choice."

He looked at his dad and thought 'what a wanker' but didn't say it, though he wanted to. "Can I have a pizza?"

Aaron said, "Have what you want, Son."

Luke rolled his eyes and decided on a pepperoni. Food and drinks were ordered and the menus were taken away.

There was silence for what felt like forever, when Luke chipped in, "So, what were you all doing last night? It got a bit noisy, didn't it? I heard Amanda shouting at you, Dad."

"Oh, nothing Luke, just dad and daughter stuff." He looked at Beth to see her change a lovely shade of red.

"You alright, Mum, you've gone all red?" Luke chuckled.

"Just the heat, Luke, you know I don't like it too hot," Beth replied, trying to brush it off.

Beth and Aaron glanced at each other and hoped they had got away with it. Aaron tried to change the subject.

"How's school treating you, Luke, still enjoying high school?"

Luke delivered his usual 'whatever' glare at Dad, the same look he'd given his mum earlier on. "I've been there nearly a year now. And yes, I'm still enjoying it."

Aaron looked at Luke. *Do I take this any further*, he thought.

The waitress arrived with the food, interrupting the conversation, it looked good. There was loads of beef on Aaron's plate and a huge Yorkshire pudding. Beth's steak pie was covered in thick gravy and Luke's pizza looked amazing, with steam coming off the top.

The waitress asked when the other guests were arriving and, to be honest, they'd all forgotten about Amanda and Matt. Beth looked at Aaron, puzzled, and told the waitress she would find out. Beth got her phone out to ring Amanda but decided to text. She hated people using their mobile phone in a restaurant.

Hi Amanda, just wondering where you and Matt are? We're at the Foundry waiting. Are you coming still? Mum.

She looked at Aaron and shrugged her shoulders. "Don't know, she said she was going to Matt's and I presumed they were coming here."

Luke looked smug. "This is going to be a better day than I thought."

Aaron was not too pleased with the comment and told him so. "Well, that's no dessert for you, Luke; that was awful."

"I didn't mean it, Dad!" Luke said, but Aaron knew different.

It was about three o'clock when they decided to leave. Beth tried to text Amanda again, telling them that they'd finished at the Foundry Inn, and were going for a walk in Poole Park.

Ring us, tell us your plans, love you.
Mum XX.

Walked round the lake and Luke played in the adventure play area. There was a cricket match on, so all three sat and watched. Aaron and Luke loved cricket, not so much for Beth, but she put up with it, so long as it kept her boys happy. Usually, Amanda was with her and they just sat and talked, but not today.

***

Aaron and Beth were sitting in the family room in Bournemouth Hospital. Amanda had spent a good two hours having blood tests, eye tests, and more. The ophthalmologist had had a good look into her eyes and a lot of questions had been asked but the main test was a CT scan, and they were now waiting nervously.

They were sitting together on a sofa with two hospital chairs across from them, a wooden table was in the middle with a cactus plant and a box of tissues on top. It was painted a clinical hospital white on the top half and a pattern wallpaper with pink flowers on the bottom.

They had left Amanda with a nurse in a side room just off the A&E department, she was so tired and had just fallen asleep. Luke was with Grandma and Grandad Simpson in Lower Parkstone. He was only four, so really had no idea what was going on.

The door opened and the doctor and nurse who had been looking after Amanda walked in. He came over to Aaron and Beth and shook their hands and the nurse followed suit. They sat down opposite. From the expression on his face, it didn't look good. He had a folder on his lap, opened it and looked at them.

"My name is Dr Hussain and this is Sister Beverly. As you know, we've done lots of tests. The initial blood tests were inconclusive. When the ophthalmologist had a look at Amanda's eyes, he did see something there and suggested a CT scan. I'll be performing the scan, so will follow Amanda down shortly. Once the scan has been completed, we'll meet again here and we'll discuss the results and answer any questions that you have."

Amanda was taken down for a CT scan and returned to the side room on the ward. After about an hour, Aaron and Beth met with Dr Hussain and Sister Beverly back in the Relatives' Room.

Dr Hussain reviewed the folder and then turning to them, "I'm afraid there's no easy way to tell you this, we have found a little mass on Amanda's brain."

He paused to allow them to react, there was silence. Aaron panicked, not understanding what had really been said and a little confused.

"Where is it? How big is it? Is it cancerous? Oh God, is she going to die?"

Beth started shaking, and Aaron got hold of her, looking at Dr Hussain for answers. Dr Hussain reassured them that it was early days yet and they had to do some more tests before they knew the outcome.

"I need to go to her!" Beth exclaimed and dashed to the ward.

Chapter 3

Beth had still not heard from Amanda. They drove home in silence. Luke dashed out to use his newly cut house key and clambered to his room. He'd been allowed a house key since starting high school.

Beth shouted up the stairs, "Are you back, Amanda?" She waited for a reply; there was nothing, absolute silence.

Aaron had to be up early for a meeting in Basingstoke, so thought it would be better to have a shower that evening. Beth was sorting the quiche and salad out and was setting the table for four, when it clicked, where was Amanda? She hadn't returned her text. Beth glanced at her phone, nothing. It was nearly 7 pm, Amanda knew they ate about this time on a Sunday.

She dialled her number and waited, it went straight onto answer phone. *What was that girl playing at,* she thought.

Beth went to the en-suite to talk to Aaron, who was just drying himself off. She explained that Amanda hadn't replied to her messages and that she was a little worried.

"Give her an hour, she's a big girl now, she's probably forgotten the time. You remember what it was like when we were young? We did the same. She's with Matt, isn't she? Go in there, give him a ring, find out what's happening."

Beth tried. Matt's phone was just ringing and ringing, it then went to voicemail. This got Beth even more anxious. Where were they? Beth stuck her head round the bathroom door again.

"There's no answer from Matt and now I'm very worried."

"Give it till 8, she'll be back," Aaron said while shaving.

Suddenly, Beth's mobile rang, she scrambled to get it and nearly missed answering. She could see it was Matt ringing.

"Hi Beth, you rang?"

"Hi Matt, can I speak to Amanda please, she's not returning any of my texts or phone calls. She left this morning in a mood, saying she was coming to yours."

There was a long pause. "I haven't seen her today, she texted me last night, something about falling out with Aaron. I haven't heard from her since, I've been at footie all afternoon and I'm in town at the King's Head with a few of the lads."

Beth asked, "Have you spoken to her today?"

Matt said, "Do you know, I haven't and that's strange because she always rings me to find out what I'm up to. Now, you've got me worried."

Beth said, "She knows we eat at 7 on a Sunday."

Matt looked at the clock over the bar and noticed it was 7:45 pm.

"She might have gone to Maggie's; do you want me to ring her and find out?" Matt asked.

Beth thought for a moment and replied, "No, it's alright, Matt, I'll ring Maggie. If she is, it wouldn't only be her dad she's fallen out with."

Beth found Maggie's number on her mobile and rang her, it went straight to answer phone.

"Fuck," said Beth, annoyed. "Where is she?"

Aaron could only hear one side of the conversation, and looked at Beth for answers. Beth looked pale.

"What is it?" Aaron asked, concerned. Beth told him what had been said.

Aaron went quiet. "Are you sure Matt hasn't heard from her?"

"What do you think? I misunderstood what he was saying?" Beth looked angry.

"I don't think he would lie, do you?" Aaron shrugged.

By this time, Luke had heard some of the conversation, he'd been sitting on the stairs, which he did a lot. Luke appeared at the doorway, asking, "What's going on?" Sitting by the breakfast bar, he looked at his mum for answers. He noticed the worried look on both the parents' faces and started to ask questions. He too had noticed that his sister wasn't there.

Aaron looked at Luke, trying to make light of the situation, just saying, "Amanda was late getting home but I'm sure she's on her way. Probably forgotten the time. I think it's time you went to bed, have you finished your homework?"

"Yes," said Luke. "I'm not going to bed until Amanda is home."

Beth just looked up at Luke. "Go to bed Luke, you've got school tomorrow." She looked at the clock again. "My God, it's nearly 9 o'clock, where is she?" She looked at Aaron again.

Luke stomped out of the kitchen, mumbling, "It's not fair, I always miss the good stuff."

Aaron looked at Beth. "Have you rung Ruth? I'm sure she will be able to tell you something."

Ruth was Maggie's mum.

"In all the confusion, I didn't even think of that." Beth picked up her phone.

Ruth and Beth had known each other since junior school and had grown up being best friends, going through all the good and bad that life had thrown at them. Ruth had been her maid of honour at her wedding to Aaron, and Beth was maid of honour when Ruth married Jack.

They were all the best of friends and could tell each other anything. Ruth was there when Amanda was born. Aaron had cried his eyes out, and Ruth was just as bad. Beth remembered how Amanda had problems breathing at first, and there were frantic movements in the delivery room, with a doctor rushing in to get the first breath of life out of her. It was such a relief when they all heard Amanda crying for the first time. She was perfect.

***

Beth looked at Aaron, he could tell from her face that there wasn't an answer; she was breaking up inside and he knew he had to sort this out. Did he wait and see if she turned up later? He'd been saying that for the last two hours and nothing had happened.

Aaron was deep in thought and quickly remembered, "What about her other friends, what's that other girl called? I can't remember her name, she was here last weekend. Maggie was here as well, the three of them went into Bournemouth to do some window shopping, God, what's she called?"

He was still thinking when Beth shouted out, "Nickie, that's it."

She opened her phone and found Chrissie's number and pressed call. Ruth and Chrissie had helped in a fund raising event to raise money for the Brain Tumour Charity, they had trained and completed a Mud Run in Finsbury Park London last April. It had taken months of training, but they had done it and raised nearly £2,500 in the process. Chrissie answered straight away.

"Hi love, you OK."

Beth gave a little laugh and proceeded to tell Chrissie the problem she had got. Chrissie was quiet, Beth could almost hear her brain ticking. Finally, she said she would go and have a word with Nickie and see if she had seen Amanda today. Beth could hear Chrissie going upstairs, and a mumbled conversation going on, then she came back.

"Beth, I'm sorry Nickie hasn't seen or heard from her today. You say her phone's switched off?" Chrissie asked.

Beth's voice started to crack, "I've rung her, no answer, and she's not returning my texts. I'm getting a bit scared now, I don't want to think the worst, but I am." Beth couldn't hold it any longer and broke into tears.

"I'm on my way round, see you in half an hour."

Chrissie didn't give Beth the chance to reply, the phone went dead. Aaron asked if Nickie had seen her. He knew Nickie hadn't from the look on her face.

"Come here," he said, and tried to comfort her but it wasn't working. "It's going to be alright, Beth." Holding her on her shoulders and watching the tears making her mascara run down her cheeks.

Beth just looked at him and said, "How do you know? She could have been in an accident, she could have been attacked, she could be in a ditch, injured, all alone and frightened. How do you know?"

All of a sudden, it hit Aaron. He hadn't taken this seriously. He had just thought she was a bit late coming home, but it was three hours now and she'd left in a right mood about 11 that morning. No one had heard from her and no one had seen her. He looked at Beth. "Where is our Amanda?"

The doorbell rang and Aaron for some reason thought it might be Amanda, but why would she be ringing the doorbell? Stupid thought. He opened it to find Matt there.

"Is she back? I was worried when Beth rang me, I couldn't stop thinking about Amy." It was always strange to hear her being called Amy, to her friends that was her name but to them, it had always been Amanda.

"Come in Matt, no, she hasn't come home yet, we're getting worried now."

Aaron and Matt walked through the lounge and into the kitchen where Beth was sitting at the breakfast bar. Matt noticed that Beth had been crying, but he didn't know what to say, he just sat next to her, quiet. There was a long pause where the three off them just looked at each other and said nothing. All of a sudden, Matt got up and said, "I'm making a cuppa, anyone else want one?" looking at them both.

He thought this might help; both Aaron and Beth said no, but he made them one anyway, putting it on the breakfast bar next to Beth and Aaron. You could see they were not on the same planet because they both started drinking.

The doorbell went again, and Beth got up to go, but Aaron said, "I'll get it."

As he got to the door, he saw Luke sitting on the stairs. "What's going on?" He asked. "Why is Mum crying? Who's in the kitchen?"

Aaron opened the door and Ruth, Jack and Chrissie stood with a concerned look on their faces. "Any news?" Ruth asked. "Chrissie rang me up, said she was coming round and I asked her to pick us up on the way."

Aaron looked at them all and just said, "Come in, we're in the kitchen." They all walked to the kitchen with Luke following close behind, as they entered, Beth took one look at her best friends and burst into tears. Ruth and Chrissie just went over and embraced her.

Jack looked at Aaron with his arms open to say, do you want one? He declined the offer. Jack then said, "Has anyone thought to ring Poole or Bournemouth Hospital, I know it's not nice to think anything could have happened to Amanda but it's worth a try."

Aaron was on his phone in an instant, thinking, why haven't I done this sooner, but you don't think, do you? When he got off the phone, they all knew that it was bad, she wasn't at either hospital.

Beth looked at the ceiling and then at Aaron and just screamed, "Where is my baby girl?"

There was a hive of activity in the house, with police everywhere. It had been Matt that suggested they ring the police and everyone had agreed, but it was with a heavy heart the realisation that something may have happened to Amanda. Aaron was in the lounge, trying to explain what had happened that day. It seemed that he was the only one who was calm enough to talk. Beth was a mess and was being consoled by Ruth and Chrissie. Luke just looked lost and tearful.

Aaron was talking to Detective Inspector Steven Walters. Walters had been in the police force for over 25 years, and was considered one of the best Detective Inspectors in Bournemouth. Six foot two or thereabouts, and had a nice smile, his face lit up whenever he did. A stickler for doing the right thing, both in his private life and his police work.

He had been called in because the initial officer thought this was going to be a serious case. It was just a feeling he had, he'd had experience in missing person's cases and to him, this one just rang bells in his head.

"Mr Simpson, what's your first name?" Asked DI Walters.

"Aaron," he replied.

Walters looked at him and saw he was finding this difficult. "Is it OK if I call you Aaron?" Walters asked.

Aaron looked up and said, "No problem, that's my name."

Walters looked around the room and asked who the other people were in the house. Aaron looked, and pointed out who everyone was and watched as he took notes.

"Can I ask how long you think your daughter's been missing?"

Aaron thought a moment and replied, "She left about 11 o'clock this morning, in a mood. Beth and Amanda had a bit of a disagreement, nothing too big, just mother/daughter stuff."

Walters looked over at Beth, to see how she was holding up, and turned to Aaron, and told him he had arranged for a liaison officer to come and be with them, to help, and answer any questions they might want answering.

"You say Mum and Amanda had a row this morning, what was it about?"

Aaron looked at Beth, she was starting to come round a little, be more composed, so Aaron suggested he ask his wife.

Walters walked over to Beth. Chrissie saw him coming and stepped to one side, Ruth stayed, holding her hand, not wanting to let go. This was her best friend, she needed her more than anything now. Walters looked at Beth, shook her hand.

"Beth, right? You can call me Steve. We are going to do everything we can to find Amanda. I'm sorry to ask but I need to know, your husband said you had a row with Amanda this morning, what was it about?"

Beth looked a bit taken aback. "It was nothing, it was really between Amanda and Luke, I'd suggested that we all go out for Sunday lunch and that included Matt, Amanda's boyfriend, Luke hit the roof, said he didn't want to come, hated Matt because he had broken the controller for his Xbox."

"Amanda came back, defending Matt by arguing it shouldn't have been on the floor in the first place, but swearing at him quite badly. It got a little out of hand, and I told Amanda I was not having language like that in this house, she just looked at us all and walked out, saying she was off to Matt's. That was it, usual family argument."

Walters turned to his left and saw DS Sally Hudson, his partner, who always worked with him on these sorts of cases. Sally was in her thirties, slim, had an

OK figure, according to Walters. She had been in the police force for about fifteen years, she came into the force as a graduate and, finally becoming a DI three years ago, and that's when she was paired off with Walters.

She had dark hair, and was tall, about the same height as Walters, they were always having a joke about who was the tallest. He noticed she was writing in her handbook.

"Did you get all that down, Sally?" Sally looked up and nodded. "This is DS Sally Hudson, my partner, she'll be working the case with me. Sally is a very experienced detective and is an expert on missing persons."

DI Walters looked at Beth and Aaron and said he had to ask them some more questions that may sound ridiculous but they would help them find Amanda.

He looked at Beth and asked, "Has Amanda ever done this before?"

Beth looked shocked. Aaron shouted, "No, Amanda's a good girl."

DI Walter looked at them both. "I have to ask, sorry. Can you remember what she was wearing?"

Beth looked at the detective and was trying to remember when Luke jumped in and reeled off, "White tank top t-shirt, blue denim shorts and her Nike white trainers."

Beth added, "White trainer socks with a blue trim."

"Did she have a bag with her?" Walters asked.

Beth replied, "It was her small duffel bag, the ones that go over both shoulders. It was denim like her shorts."

"Have you got a recent photo of Amanda? And we'll need her toothbrush if that's OK?" Walters asked. At this point, Beth lost it, she realised where this was going.

Ruth, who was closest, grabbed Beth and Aaron and ran over to comfort her, saying, "Beth, they have to ask these questions, they need them to watch for her, out and about."

Beth got even more agitated and just shouted out, "It's so they can identify her when they find her."

Aaron grabbed her and looked into her eyes, he was trying to be strong. "Listen, stop thinking that way. It's not going to bring Amanda back, is it? We have to be strong, all of us, now let the detectives do what they are good at, let them find Amanda."

She fell into Aaron's arms and sobbed. After calming Beth down, Aaron went to a drawer in the lounge and found a recent photo of Amanda, it was one of her graduation from Bournemouth School for Girls. Amanda had done really well. Matt went into his wallet and pulled out a picture of Amanda and him at the Dolphin Centre, smiling and looking so much in love, he handed it to Hudson. Hudson took them both and thanked them. Aaron asked Luke to go and get Amanda's toothbrush.

"What's all that about, why they need her toothbrush?" asked Luke.

"They just do, Luke, now can you get it, please?" Aaron said it between his teeth. DS Walters watched Luke turn, open the door and heard him stomping upstairs.

"Can I ask, do you have her mobile number, just for our records?" He looked at Aaron. "And the names of any friends she has and places she might frequent?"

Aaron and Beth looked at each other and were confused, they really didn't know where their daughter went or frequented. Aaron looked over at Matt for help, knowing Amanda spent most of her time with him. DI Walters looked over a Matt and just said, "We can get those details later, is that OK with you, Matt?"

"No problem."

Matt looked sheepish and worried at both Aaron and Beth, but especially at DI Walters.

Chapter 4

At Bournemouth station, DI Walters and the team were starting to put a plan together. Their first concern was to get this out to the media as soon as possible.

By the time, they had got back to the station and had got all the information they could from Beth and Aaron and all the others present, dawn was breaking. DS Hudson looked at her watch, saw it was 4:25 am, she knew everyone was exhausted, but also knew that the first 48 hours were crucial in any investigation, looked at Walters, asking, "What do you think?"

Walters didn't answer straight away. He walked up to a white board on the wall, pinned the picture of Amanda at the top, wrote her name underneath and turned to Hudson, saying, "I don't like the look of this one but we have to assume she is still with us, and that is how we will carry on."

"I want this on the 6 am news. Do a press release now, you've got all the details there. I know we have put out a description for our uniforms to be on the lookout, and patrols are all over the place, problem is we have no clues yet of where she is and if anything has happened to her."

Bournemouth police have just made a statement saying that a sixteen-year-old girl went missing yesterday, Amanda Simpson of Parkstone, Poole was last seen leaving her house at about 11 am on Sunday morning, she was wearing a White T-shirt and Blue denim shorts, white Nike trainers, white socks with a blue trim and carrying a denim over the shoulder bag.

She is 5ft 6in. Blonde hair and Caucasian. If you recognise her from the photograph or have any information, please contact Bournemouth police station on 01202 222222 and ask for DI Walters, or contact Crime-stoppers on 0800 555 111 Anonymity is guaranteed.

There was a knock on Aaron's door, he ran thinking it was Amanda, but of course, why would she knock? He opened it to find DI Walter and DS Hudson standing, looking quite sombre.

"Have you found her? Please say you have, this is killing us." Aaron was looking hopeful.

"Can we come in, please?" said Walters. Aaron walked into the house followed by the two detectives, shutting the door.

"I'm sorry Aaron, so far, we haven't got anything, but it's only been 24 hours, too early to say. Where's Mrs Simpson?"

Aaron looked at the ceiling and pointed.

"I can't imagine that you've slept much," Walters said.

"Most people had gone by 7 am, we saw the news at 6 and Beth more or less collapsed and I put her to bed. Ruth said, "do you want me to stay?" And I said we would be OK, and thanked her for being there for Beth."

DS Hudson looked at Aaron and asked, "How are you coping?"

"I know she's not here, I can't get my head around that. I'm in limbo, it hurts so much, but I have to stay strong for Beth and Luke." Aaron looked at Walters.

"How's Luke managing?" asked Hudson.

Aaron replied, "He's just sitting there watching and listening, really not saying much. He put himself to bed when Matt left earlier. I know it's not nice to say, and I shouldn't, but Luke's thinking he's got a day off school, which I suppose he has."

"Can I ask about Luke? Does he get on with Amanda?"

Aaron was a bit confused and looked at DI Walters and said, "Why are you asking about Luke? He has nothing to do with Amanda's disappearance. OK, they have their moments but they're brother and sister; that happens. He's just as concerned, as we all are."

DS Hudson looked at him. "You said he was cross with Matt breaking his Xbox and being in his bedroom?"

Aaron started to raise his voice, "Maybe you should ask Beth or Luke about it. The problem I've got is that I'm not here much due to my job."

"And why is that?" Walters asked.

"I work for IBM, I'm a computer programmer, and I have to go where I'm wanted, be it in the UK or abroad. If there is a problem with some software, I go and sort it out," replied Aaron.

"So really, you wouldn't know if there was a problem between them?" asked Walters.

Hudson added, "Does Luke get on with Matt?"

Aaron shrugged. "Most of the time, but lately, there does seem to be a strained atmosphere between them, I don't know why. When Amanda met Matt, Matt and Luke got on pretty well, on the occasions I saw, the three of them were always together, laughing, playing tricks on each other, generally having a good time, but when Amanda had had enough, she asked Luke to disappear. I don't think that Luke understood that Matt had come round to see Amanda, not him."

Hudson continued, "Do you think this might have made Luke angry and blame Matt?"

"For what?" Aaron said.

Hudson looked at Walters and thought, *we need to talk to Luke.* Aaron looked at both of them, confused.

Suddenly, the door opened with Beth coming in looking like death warmed up. "What's all the noise?"

Looking round the room, she saw the two detectives. She went into a fit of uncontrollable shaking. "What's happened, where is she, have you found her? Please tell me you have."

Aaron came over and got Beth to sit on the sofa and tried to calm her down. It didn't work.

"Why are you here, shouldn't you be out there looking for my daughter? She could be lying in a ditch injured, bleeding, we need to find her," Beth said loudly.

Hudson sat next to Beth and assured her that was what they were doing.

"The problem is, all we've got is we know she left here about 11am yesterday morning, but after that, we have no idea where she went," Walters was trying to placate Beth.

Just then, there was a knock on the door, Walters went to answer it and both Aaron and Beth could hear a conversation going on at the door. Walters returned with a woman, she was not dressed in a police uniform, she was about 40 years old, slim, with a mop of red hair and conservatively dressed.

Walters introduced them, "Aaron, Beth, I'd like you to meet April Smith. April is going to stay with you, if that's alright, April is your liaison officer and will keep you informed of any new info or leads that might come up, and also look after both of you and get you through this."

"You can ask her anything, if she knows the answer, she'll tell you and if she doesn't, she'll find it. April is very experienced and has helped lots of people in this and other situations."

Looked at both of them and saw the pain they were going through. She'd seen it so many times before, but she knew what she had to do, keep it calm.

"Hi Aaron, hi Beth, I know this is not easy. Is it alright if I call you by your first names?"

Beth looked up at Aaron as if to say, you answer.

"Yes, of course," said Aaron.

April again looked at them both and said exactly what DI Walters had said but added, "Don't worry, we will find her."

"Is it alright if we have a look in Amanda's room? It might give us a clue as to what might have happened and where she's gone."

Walters was looking at April like she was dirt. Beth pointed to the kitchen door and told them that it was at the top of the stairs and the first door on the right. They got to the room and were surprised at how clean and organised it was.

"My God," DS Hudson said. "My room never looked like this when I was 16."

Walters looked at her and laughed, saying, "Now that I can believe. Excuse me, Sally," looking daggers at Walters.

"I'm sure you were a teenager back in the day, when was that, I was told it was the fifties." Giving him a cheeky smile.

"Just watch yourself, Hudson, I know we have a good relationship, but don't take it too far." He smiled and wagging his finger, still smiling, said, "And respect your superiors." They went through all the drawers and cupboards not finding anything of interest. Sally was looking at a montage of photos of her with Matt and her friends. DI Walters found a box on top of the wardrobe, pulled it down and put it on the bed.

"Look at this, Hudson."

"What you found? Oh interesting." She watched him slide the top off the box.

Inside were photos of Amanda and Matt all over Poole and Bournemouth having a great time, photos of Mum and Dad and of the whole family, but underneath, hiding, was a small book, it looked like a notebook, no, it was a dairy, Amanda's. Great, they would read that back at the station.

DI Walters and Hudson said their goodbyes to Beth and Aaron, then Walters asked if April had a minute. She followed them outside. Walters turned round, trying to keep calm and looked her straight in the face.

"Why did you say that, 'don't worry, we will find her.' You know we try not to give them too much hope." Walters looked angry.

April just looked right back at him and calmly said, "You do things your way and I will do things my way, I don't tell you how to do your job, don't tell me how to do mine."

April walked back inside. Walters and Hudson got in their car. Walters, looking at Hudson, saying, "Bitch."

***

Amanda had no idea where she was. Nearby, she could hear trains and cars. There was a funny smell, like dead rats. *Where am I, what the hell has happened?* She tried to remember, but couldn't.

She felt wet, and realised she was lying in a puddle of water. She tried to get up, but couldn't. She looked around and her eyes focused on walls, dark stone walls with green and brown moss all over them. A light ahead, coming from the bottom of a door.

Then the realisation hit her, she was tied up, her hands behind her back and her legs tied together. She screamed in panic, and started to sob. *I need to think, think Amanda. What's happened? Why am I here?* She tried to remember, but it was all blank. She couldn't stop sobbing and screamed again, and again and again. "Why is no one coming? Someone help me!"

Chapter 5

Walters and Hudson arrived back at the station and Walters' first words were, "Right, what have we got, anything, anything we can use?" He looked around the room to see faces with blank expressions.

"Have we got any leads from the news bulletin, Crime-stoppers? What is wrong with people, surely someone has seen her, seen something, a sixteen-year-old girl doesn't just disappear in broad daylight at 11 on a Sunday morning. Right, we know she was going to see Matt, her boyfriend."

"Detective Ross, I need you and Detective Moore to go out there and walk from the Simpson House, to Matt's house in Westbourne. He has a flat above Simply Beds on Poole Road I gather it's not far from the Simpson's house. What's his surname?" Walters looked at Moore.

Moore looked at his notepad and called out, "Fisher."

Walters nodded. "I want you to be on the lookout for CCTV cameras, go into shops, pubs anywhere you might think have CCTV. Let's find this girl. I'm told that we have a search party going out this afternoon?"

"Yes," said Detective Moore.

"It's been on the local radio stations for anyone who can spare the time and take an hour out of their day to help the Simpsons find their daughter," Walters replied.

"It can only help. Who's organising it?"

"Police Headquarters and Dorset Search and Rescue who are experts at finding missing people," said Moore.

"Where's the meeting point?" Walters asked.

"At the Retail Park Branksome, at the top off Bournemouth Road off Ashley Road, 300 metres from the Simpson Home," Moore replied.

"Well, at least we can see something happening," said Walters. "Sally, can you get this info to April the liaison officer, so she can tell the Simpsons what's

33

going on?" He thought to himself, *I don't particularly want to talk to her at the moment.*

Hudson looked at Walters as if reading his mind, *you'll have to sooner or later.*

***

Matt thought, *how was he going to get out of this?* He'd told Amanda that he loved her and in his own little way, he did. They had had a blazing row three days ago. She wanted to know where he had been on Wednesday night. She had tried to ring him, text him, but couldn't reach him.

He hoped that telling her he was at a mate's flat, they'd had a few to drink and he had fallen asleep on the couch and his phone was out of juice would make it all OK. It didn't, she didn't believe him.

But, even with the way things were between them, he wanted to know where she was. He was trying to think of all the places she might go, the park, the cinema, that coffee bar in the Dolphin Centre, but to him, they all seemed a dead end. Was his lie the cause of her disappearance? He hoped not.

When Aaron heard about the search, he wanted to go straight away, so did Beth and Luke. April stopped them.

"Look, I know you want to go and search for Amanda, that's understandable, but can I suggest that at least one of you stays here, just in case Amanda comes back? It won't be nice for her if the house is empty." She looked at Beth kindly. "Beth, you're not in a fit state to go anywhere."

Beth looked at Aaron, and he nodded in agreement.

Aaron rubbed her arm gently. "Love, April is right, you haven't slept properly for over 24 hours. You need to be here for Amanda. I'll ring every half hour to tell you if there is any progress, I promise."

Beth looked defeated and started crying again, Aaron went to cuddle her but Luke got there, and before he could even move, Luke had grabbed hold of his mum and squeezed her tight, saying, "Don't worry, Mum, I'll stay with you. I want to. Let's have a cup of tea. I'll even make it. Yes, me."

Aaron and April looked at each other. April said, "Well, that's sorted then, and don't worry, Luke, I'll make the tea."

Luke looked at April, scowling. "I'm quite capable of making tea," and walked to the kitchen with a plan in his head.

"We could do with more Lukes in the world," said April.

Beth agreed to stay but made Aaron stick to his word, every 30 minutes or else. Aaron looked across and tried to smile. "I will, I promise."

He picked the car keys up from the coffee table, said his goodbyes and set off for the retail park.

***

When Aaron arrived at the search, he noticed that only a few people had turned up. He went to the makeshift tent erected by the Dorset Search and Rescue team and made himself known.

"What can I do, where are we starting? There doesn't seem to be many here."

In the tent was a man with a ruddy look, a long ginger beard with hair to match, and was wearing a beanie hat. He was dressed like he was going to climb a mountain. *He was big*, thought Aaron.

"Hi there, I'm sorry I didn't get your name," asked Aaron.

"I'm Rob Clark, leader of the search party." Rob looked, wondering who the hell was standing there.

Aaron looked at him and saw that underneath all that hair was a kindly face of a man who cared. "Oh, sorry," said Aaron. "I'm the father of Amanda, it's my daughter that's gone missing."

Rob looked at Aaron, he looked exhausted/unstable, but he knew there was no way of stopping him taking part in the search. Rob started to say how sorry he was, but his team were there to search for and rescue Amanda if needed.

"Just tell me what I can do and where you want me," Aaron interrupted.

Rob said it was too early to start the search, the rest of the team were on their way and of course, there were the public volunteers yet to arrive.

"How long do you think?" asked Aaron.

Rob looked at his watch and said, "I would think it will be about an hour or so, but that still gives us at least four hours of daylight, and we will go on all night if we have to."

Aaron looked around at the people, gathering to help and he felt tears starting to form. *Hold yourself together*, he told himself. "Thanks everyone," he managed before he had to turn away.

***

Ruth heard the doorbell ring and walked from the kitchen where she was preparing tea for herself and Jack, her husband. He was at work, a sales director for a large car dealership in Bournemouth. He earned good money and that meant that Ruth was a stay at home wife and mother and that was how Jack liked it. He was a bit of a chauvinist at times, a loveable rogue. Ruth had met Jack when she was buying her first car.

She'd worked hard for that car, saved all her Saturday job wages, working as a domestic in a care home, about £500 in the end. She loved her job and couldn't wait to buy the car she had always wanted.

This was her third visit to the garage, first to have a look and choose the car, second to pay for it, and now to pick it up after it had had its MOT and a few adjustments. Jack had noticed her the first time she'd come and had made a beeline to help her.

They had both fancied each other straight away, and Jack plucked up the courage to ask her out, and they had been together ever since. They had one daughter, Margaret, known to most as Maggie. Ruth remembered driving off in her light blue Ford Focus, thinking, *this has been a good day.*

Ruth could see a silhouette through the glass pane and opened the door.

"Hi Ruth," said Aaron.

He was looking haggard.

"You OK, what are you doing here?" she asked.

She could see he was near to breaking, and pulled him into a hug. He laid his head on her shoulder and started sobbing. Ruth pulled him away and looked into his eyes and said, "They'll find her, you know that, don't you?"

Aaron just couldn't help himself and pulled Ruth closer and gave her a kiss, Ruth didn't stop him, she knew he was hurting but she also knew she was being used. Ruth had broken off their affair two months ago and Aaron had taken it badly.

He'd offered to leave Beth, but he'd said that so many times over the last three years. She would always say, "Your needle's stuck again." He pleaded with her, said he loved her, she knew that and she loved him, they had even made love for the last time, she supposed for old time's sake. "Why did I do that?"

It was over but she had to be there for him, didn't she, she couldn't just tell him to go, there would always be something there, she still had feelings.

"Aaron, stop," Ruth said. "We can't do this."

Aaron dropped his arms and slowly pulled back, still looking into her eyes. "Ruth, I know I've cocked it up, I've got to live with that."

The front door opened, Jack walked in. They stepped apart quickly.

"Are you alright, mate, I'm here if you want to talk, if you want anything, all you have to do is ask," said Jack. Jack walked over to Aaron and gave him a hug.

Funnily enough, Aaron found it quite soothing and squeezed Jack tightly. Jack asked, "Do you want a drink, tea, coffee, beer? Haven't you offered Aaron a drink yet, Ruth?"

Aaron cut in, "It's alright, Jack. I've only been here five minutes. Actually, it's you I've come to see."

"What do you need, mate? Anything. Just ask." He could see Arron was a mess.

Aaron went to sit down on the sofa and Ruth sat on a chair nearby.

"I don't know if you've heard, but the police are having a search for Amanda this afternoon. We're all meeting at the Retail Park Branksome. I was hoping you would come and help and, in a way, be there for me if the worst comes to the worst?"

Jack looked at Aaron and replied, "I had heard it on the radio and that's why I've come home earlier."

Ruth looked at Aaron, concerned. "Are you going to be alright? You look awful."

Aaron didn't like the way Ruth had said that and rudely replied, "Well, thanks for that."

Jack left it, knowing Aaron was going through the mill.

"Right, I'm going upstairs, get out of this suit. Be five minutes."

Jack left them alone. Ruth just sat there, saying nothing. Eventually, Aaron said, "Sorry for being a prick. I didn't mean to say it like that."

"It's OK, you're stressed, just be careful. I'll be thinking of you, of you both and Amanda."

There was another pause.

"Do you want that drink?" asked Ruth just as Jack was coming down the stairs.

"Right Ruth, see you whenever. I'll give you a ring if there are any developments."

He bent down and kissed Ruth on the cheek and turned to Aaron. "Your car or mine?"

Aaron said, "Yours, of course, it's better than mine."

Ruth shouted out, "You two keep safe, please."

The light was fading through the edges of the door. Amanda couldn't remember if this was the second night she had been there, or was it longer? She started to shake with fear again, that dream had come back again, but this time it wasn't in her sleep. It was like it was in front of her. Three men standing round a body looking down.

"What a way to go, who could have done that to a young girl like that?"

She got up and walked to the men and looked over their shoulders. That girl looked like her. Same t-shirt, her new white Nike trainers, her white trainer socks with the blue trim. Knickers and blue denim shorts lying near her head. She then noticed something round the girl's neck, a bra? Was that really her? She closed her eyes, and when she opened them again, there was nothing, nothing but the dark. She screamed.

"Help me! Help me!" getting louder. "For God's sake, somebody, help me." She was confused; was it a nightmare like last time, or was it real? She tried to calm down, and let the dark lull her back to a shaky sleep.

Chapter 6

"Hi darling," said Aaron as Amanda shot upright in bed, confused, wondering where she was.

"It's OK, you're in hospital. Mummy and Daddy are here to look after you. We're here with you all the time you are in here. Getting better."

Aaron gave Amanda a big hug. Beth was finding it hard to keep it together, and Amanda saw this.

"Is Mummy alright, Daddy, why is she crying, what's wrong with me?"

"Oh, she's just upset you're in hospital and we missed going to McDonald's last night."

Amanda looked at Daddy and said, "Yes we did," crossly.

"Well, we better go today then, and that will make Mummy better, and me as well," as she looked at both Aaron and Beth, who laughed.

Just then, a nurse came in and saw them all laughing, and shouted, "Someone must have told a good joke, was it you, Amanda?" Amanda went very quiet and went under the covers.

Beth said, "Amanda that's not nice, Nurse Suzie has just come to say hello. Do you know she has been coming every hour during the night to make sure that you were alright? Don't you think that was nice of her?"

"Yes," very quietly came the reply from under the sheets.

Nurse Suzie started to get closer to the bed and leaned over, slowly peeling the bedsheets back, saying, "I bet there's a little girl under here who I know hasn't eaten for a whole day?"

Then Suzie slowly grabbed the second sheet and said, "Well, do you know what, I've brought you something to eat, and it's amazing. Do you know what it is? Even Mummy and Daddy don't know."

All of a sudden, there was a little chuckle from under the sheets. She came to the final sheet, Amanda was curled up in a tiny ball, waiting for the sheet to be pulled back, now chuckling quite a lot. Aaron and Beth were really laughing now, but Nurse Suzie crept up and slowly started to pull it all the way down to Amanda curled in that little ball.

"Oh," said Nurse Suzie. "I have a feeling that Amanda doesn't want this amazing something that I have brought for her to eat, what do you think, Mummy and Daddy?"

Beth looked at Amanda, put her hand on her back and said, "Do you know Amanda, Nurse Suzie has just shown me what it is and, wow, are you going to love it."

They could all see her head trying to turn, to try and get a glimpse of whatever it was.

"Right," said Nurse Suzie, "I'll make a deal with you, I want you to close your eyes and turn around and I want you to sit up and lean against your pillows still with your eyes shut and I will give you the tray with the special something you're going to love."

Amanda did exactly that, and was again giggling all the way through her turn. Suzie checked to make sure her eyes were closed. She told her a couple of times to remind her. She was in position.

Suzie said, "Are you ready, don't forget keep your eyes closed."

Suzie got the tray and put it on Amanda's knees and counted to three. "Open your eyes," Suzie said. And all three of them just looked at her face to see the reaction and it was magical. To us, it may have not been an amazing something, but to an eight-year-old girl who was going through hell, it was everything.

Nurse Suzie had sorted out a little teddy bear and the biggest bowl of chocolate, vanilla and strawberry ice-cream, and she'd made a friend for life. Beth's eyes filled with tears at the memory. Amanda still had that little bear upstairs on her bed. *Oh, where are you, my little girl!*

Chapter 7

DI Walters and DS Hudson were driving to Westbourne to talk to Matt Fisher, when DS Walters' mobile rang. He pressed the loudspeaker button, saying, "Walters."

"Sir, it's Glen. We've got a lead." Glen Bishop was a Detective Constable in the CID and had been given the task of going through any leads coming in, Walter started drumming the steering wheel in excitement.

"Go on, give me the details, is it any good?" asked Walters.

Glen looked at the yellow slip in his hand, rereading the text, and replied, "Well, I think it's a goer. It's from a trolley pusher, he works at that Tesco's on Poole Road, he said he thinks he saw Amanda walking past him that Sunday afternoon. He recognised her from the photograph that was on the TV bulletin this morning. He's working this afternoon, says there's no problems to you going down and having a talk."

"Sounds good to me, we're on Ashley Road at the moment, it's only ten minutes away. What's his name?"

"Cyril Parks," replied Glen.

"Thanks for that, here's hoping," said Walters.

"Yeah, good hunting," Bishop said.

They arrived at the Tesco's ten minutes later, and saw a frail bloke who maybe looked in his sixties, pushing trolleys, there must have been twenty to twenty-five in a line. He was well wrapped up with what looked like a raincoat in yellow with a luminous orange stripe down the back, front and on the arms, a thick scarf, beanie hat and a good pair of boots.

"Good God," said Walters, "you wouldn't have thought he could have pushed one, never mind all of them."

"Putting you to shame, is he Steve?" laughed Hudson.

"Ha, ha, ha. I'll have you know, in my day, I'd have been able to push twice as much." Walters turned to look at Hudson.

"Twice as much, yeah. Oh, I'm sorry, have I hit a nerve?"

Hudson just looked at the trolley man and got out of the car and was walking in his direction. Hudson was just laughing, but knew she had to stop, they had a job to do, but it was nice to wind him up, sometimes.

"Cyril Parks?" Hudson was asking this guy, who was just about to slam the twenty-five trolleys into a bay cordoned off from the cars.

"Who's asking?" said Cyril as he turned around and looked at them.

Walters got his warrant card out, showing Cyril his credentials and Hudson did the same.

"My name is DI Steven Walters and this is my colleague, DS Sally Hudson. We are looking into the disappearance of Amanda Simpson and have been told that you have some information that might be able to help us."

"Well, I don't know if it will, I was watching yesterday's morning news before I came to work and I thought, what were her parents going through, it must be hell for them. Then the picture of this girl came on and I thought, wait a minute, I think I've seen her somewhere, thought about it and it came to me."

"I was doing my usual, picking trolleys up as I walked around the carpark, I was going down the bottom end near that wall." He pointed to a small red-bricked wall that went all the way along the carpark.

"And what did you see?" asked Hudson.

"Well, at first, I thought, it can't be that girl they had shown on the TV yesterday morning, so I looked again, she was wearing the clothes that they'd described, and do you know what made me think, 'Yes, it is'?" Cyril was looking at Walters.

"No, what was that?"

"It was the white trainer socks with the frilly blue trim, and of course, the blond hair, and she just looked very pretty."

Walters looked hard at Cyril and for one moment, he was thinking, had he got something to do with her disappearance? He put it out of his mind very quickly.

"Can you remember what time this was?" Walters gave Hudson a look of surprise and a lift of his shoulders, Hudson was wondering what the hell he was doing.

"I would say about 1 to 1:30 pm because I was thinking of my lunch break, which I usually take between these times, and this was my last sweep before I went to lunch," Cyril replied.

"When you saw her, did you notice anyone following her, anyone looking suspicious, anyone who looked out of place?" Walters hoped he would have, but he was sure he was admiring Amanda too much to be thinking about anybody following her.

"No, I didn't, I was just thinking I need to report this, so I rang you up on the helpline. I hope I did the right thing, Detective Inspector." Cyril was looking like he was thinking, and it was hurting.

"Well, if anything comes to mind, here's my card, it has the Detectives' Room number, and my mobile number, just ring me, anytime. Day or night."

"Will do, I hope it helps." Cyril was smiling.

"It does. Thanks," said Hudson.

Hudson was scanning the area and saw that there were CCTV cameras. She asked Cyril, "Now, I see you have CCTV, is there any chance we can have a look at the other day and watch what happened?" Hudson was pointing to them.

Cyril looked up at them as well and said, "I don't see there would be a problem, but it's not for me to say, you'd have to speak to the store manager, he's the only one who can help you with that one."

"What's the manager called?" asked Walters.

Cyril replied, "Mr Andrew Berlinski."

"Thanks again Cyril, you've been a great help. Where do I find the manager?"

Walter looked at Cyril. "You are best going to Customer Service Desk, and getting a call out for him, it's better than traipsing round the store." Cyril was pointing to the front entrance.

"OK Cyril, if I can ask you to give your details to DS Hudson, we'll leave you alone to get back to your work, there does seem to be a backlog." Walters was looking at all the trolleys everywhere. "Don't forget, think of anything, ring me."

"Will do."

Andrew Berlinski was walking up to the Customer Service Desk. Walters knew it was him, he was wearing a very nice suit, bluey grey with silver stripes running down the length, shiny black shoes, a white shirt and a Tesco's tie. He was medium built, about six feet, with brown hair. He looked to be in his thirties. He introduced himself and the detectives showed their warrant cards.

They explained why they were there and there was a look of defeat on his face.

"We have a problem with your request, it's not that we can't facilitate your request, it's just that we can't get into the digital CD box until midnight, that's when it transfers over to the next one waiting to record the next day, then we can take it out. Sorry, but I can email it to you when we've got it, that would be no problem," Mr Berlinski said.

"That sound fine, we only need the scenes from about noon to 3pm last Sunday if that's OK, and if you could send it to this email address, I would be grateful. And just to verify," Walters said, "it's the carpark video we need."

"As I say, there will be no problems with that at all, you should get that by about 1 am tonight." Mr Berlinski looked at Walters and shook his hand. Hudson did the same and they walked out to the car, watching Cyril pushing a line of what must have been forty trolleys up the carpark.

Mind you, he did have someone at the front guiding them into the space for trolleys. Walters found it fascinating and said to Hudson, "I wouldn't mind a try of that someday."

Hudson laughed and looked at Walters and trying to be kind, said, "In your dreams, Steve, you would have no chance, you're not built for that sort of exercise."

Walters just looked at Sally, and said, "You know what you can do."

"I don't know but I'm sure you're going to tell me." Sally was laughing even louder.

"You can piss off, you're driving back to the station."

Walters was not taking it well. "I thought we were going to talk to Matt Fisher."

"Well, at the moment that can wait. We need to follow up on this lead. The family said she left about 11 on Sunday morning and Cyril Parks said he saw here walking past Tesco's carpark about 1 that Sunday afternoon, where was she in that two hour, what was she doing and most importantly, who was she with?"

***

Aaron and Jack arrived at the retail park at about 3:45 pm to see about 100 people, all of different ages. There was a search and rescue team, lots of police, a police truck and a couple of gazebos, with tea and coffee on the go, press and TV reporting the events. There was a man who looked official, surrounded by others looking at a big ordinance survey map of the area going right around Parkstone and on to Westbourne.

Aaron and Jack made a beeline to that gazebo, Aaron recognising Rob Clark, the main organiser of the search.

"Hello," said Aaron to Rob Clark, who looked up from the map and recognised Aaron straight away.

Rob looked at Aaron. "Hi," recognising Aaron from earlier, saying, "you'll have to excuse me, I know who you are but I can't remember your name?"

"Yes, I'm sure you've seen a lot of people since I was here earlier on. I'm Aaron Simpson, Amanda's father, and this is my friend, Jack. We're here to help in any way we can, just tell us where you want us?" Sounding more like a plea than a request. Aaron saw the map, noticed that his house was circled on it, and there were some circles on different parts of the maps, points of interest, Aaron thought.

Jack pointed at the map, and asked, "What that's circle on the centre off Westbourne?"

Aaron knew straight away. "That's where Matt lives, and that was where Amanda was going yesterday morning."

Rob looked at Aaron to see how he looked and asked him how he was coping. Aaron replied, "I'm still in a daze, still can't think this is happening, not to my daughter, and why? I just want to find her and that's why I'm here, why we're here. Just tell us what we need to do and we'll do it."

Rob was giving instruction out to certain leaders of groups who then took their troupe off to start their search. It looked to Jack like it had been done in a grid formation starting from Aaron's house and spreading out in all directions.

Rob thought it might be better if Aaron stayed at the mission hub so that if anything came in, they could take him to, for want of a better word, identify anything that was found.

Aaron's reply was swift, "No chance, I would feel like a spare part here. I have to be out there. It's the only thing I have left to do, I have to find my daughter and I really don't want to say this but," as he looked at Jack and broke into tears, "even if she is dead, or hopefully alive."

Jack held Aaron. "Don't be silly, we are going to find her."

***

There was a knock on Beth's door and Luke ran to answer it.

Beth shouted out, "No, Luke, I'll get it, don't answer the door."

But it was too late, and as the door opened, there was a frenzy of cameras and reporters, stumbling for questions and pictures. Beth went to slam the door, but Ruth managed to slip in first.

Ruth stumbled into the kitchen and shouted, "For God's sake, can't they leave you alone, they're like vultures." Beth started crying and Ruth ran across and held her.

Luke saw what was happening to Mum and ran up and hugged them both, saying, "It's alright, Mum."

Ruth got hold of Beth's head and held it in front of hers, grasping it tight, saying, "Now, stop this Beth, you have to be strong for Amanda, she could come in at any time, and she wouldn't want to see you like this, would she?"

No, thought Beth. She didn't know why but started to think about Aaron.

"Where's Aaron? He said he would ring me every half an hour, he hasn't rung me for over an hour, what's he doing, he should have rung, I'm going crazy."

Ruth held her again and said, "Something must have come up, I'm sure he will ring with what is happening soon," trying to calm Beth down.

"That's easy for you to say, you're not the one waiting with no information, and your daughter out there, who knows where."

By the time Walters and Hudson had got back to the nick, it must have been about 4 pm. When they entered the control room, they were met by the Chief Inspector, Sir Tom Burke. Sir Tom had been in the force for nearly 34 years and started in the police cadets in Norwich in 1988.

He was an honoured police officer with many distinctions and bravery awards and had played a significant role in a lot of changes to policing throughout his career. He was well-respected, and was the go-to officer to ask anything, and he meant it when he said it. He had got his knighthood for services to the police force.

Sir Tom saw DI Walters walking in and shouted, "Steve, got a minute? How's it going with the missing girl? Come to my office and give me an update, will you?"

Walter walked with Sir Tom to his office and sat on a comfy chair in front of a large polished desk with lots of files and papers, neatly set. There was a plaque with his name on the front. On the walls were painting and pictures of

Poole and Bournemouth, one of Sandbanks, Bournemouth Pier and one of the beach and sea view. There was one of him receiving his knighthood from the Queen in 2017, which he was very proud of.

"Right Steve, how is it going?" Sir Tom was looking at Steve.

"Well Sir, we have got everything in motion, uniform are doing a great job, doing the search and house-to-house near to where Amanda lives. There is a big search party at the retail park up by Bournemouth Road, corner of Ashley Road. That's starting about now. I've been told there's about 100 people there, Search and Rescue."

"Our police and our Dog Patrol and Dorset Search and Rescue are there as well. We've had our first lead in, a trolley man from Tesco's, thinks he saw Amanda walking past there about 1 to 1.30, Sunday afternoon. We're waiting for the CCTV to come in. I'm sure we will get some more in soon, someone must have seen her, it was a Sunday during the day." DI Walters finished his report.

Sir Tom looked thoughtful, and then asked, "How are the family coping?"

"Beth, the mum, is in bits, Aaron, the dad, is coping, don't know for how long, and Luke, the brother, is just looking after Mum. I don't think it's got through to him yet."

Sir Tom got up from his chair and came round to DI Walters and said to him, "I'm pleased with how the case is going so far, and if you need anything, you only need to ask. Steve, and I mean anything, we have to find this girl."

Chapter 8

Aaron and Jack had been asked if they would have a look and search round the retail park. The group charged with doing that were standing about five metres away near the tea tent.

Aaron made a face at Rob, not understanding. "Why there?" said Aaron.

Rob looked at Aaron and said, "We have to think of all avenues, your house is just over there and we know she said she was going to her boyfriend's, Matt, wasn't it? Maybe she popped into the shops to have a look before she went on, we don't know, the police are getting CCTV from the stores and they will be going through them tomorrow, but we need to look around the perimeter, in the bins, anywhere we might think she could be. Now, you said you would be OK with this. Watching your face, it doesn't seem that way."

"Oh, I'm alright, it's just getting my head around what I'm—what we are all—doing here. I see all these people here, they don't know Amanda, they don't know my family. And they are willing to come here on a Sunday early evening to help us find Amanda. Why?"

He looked at Rob for an answer. Rob looked at his chart and slowly started speaking, "Do you know, Aaron, there is a lot in the papers every day about muggings, murders, little old ladies being attacked in their homes." He slowly looked up and peered into Aaron eyes.

"The scum that do that are not here, these are the good people, the ones that care. Some of them may even know what you are going through because it could have happened to their daughters, their sons. We don't know, but I bet if you went and asked them, the reply would be, we just wanted to help, and that is it, Aaron, that is it. The good people always come out of the woodwork."

Aaron and Jack turned and walked in the direction of the first store, torch in hand, and a determination that they were going to find Amanda.

"Oh shit!" Aaron shouted. Everyone turned to look at him.

"Sorry. Sorry, I've forgotten something." Jack was shocked. Aaron didn't normally swear in public, alright, when he was with the lads, maybe, but that was not Aaron. He looked mortified.

"What have you forgotten?" asked Jack.

"I've forgotten to ring Beth."

Jack looked at Aaron and nodded. "Bollocks, I need to ring Ruth as well. Aaron, you know we're going to be in deep door-to-door, don't you?" Jack was laughing.

Aaron pulled his phone out of his pocket, Jack did the same, Aaron walked one way, Jack the other.

Aaron said, "Hi Beth."

The reply wasn't good. "Where have you been? I've been sitting here, walking round the room, Luke asking me every five minutes if I've heard anything. You promised me every thirty minutes, it's been nearly an hour and half." Beth was sounding angry.

"I'm so sorry, love, it has been frantic, with all that is going on, the police, the search and rescue team and all the people here. I just got caught up in the moment," Aaron was trying to explain.

Beth seemed to calm down a little. "So, what's been going on? What do you know? And don't lie to me."

Aaron went through everything, telling Beth what he knew, who he had been talking to, he told her about Rob and how brilliant he was and not to worry, Rob had said it was very early days yet and again not to worry.

"So, please don't panic, we will find her," Aaron said lovingly.

Aaron could hear a similar conversation going on with Jack and Ruth and just nodded at Jack to see if it was alright, he nodded back. *Good*, thought Aaron.

"Beth, I've got to go now, they're calling for the search to start."

"OK," said Beth, "but don't forget, every thirty minutes. Please, it makes me feel better, hearing your voice."

Aaron replied, "I will, I promise, I've set the alarm on my watch so I don't forget."

"Now that sounds a good idea," Beth said sarcastically.

"Love you, Beth. Tell Luke I love him too, and I'll be back when I can." Aaron was hoping that was enough.

Jack walked up and smiled.

"Everything alright?" Looking hopeful.

"Yes, everything is OK," replied Aaron.

"Ruth and Maggie are there, which can only be a great help for them all."

Jack said that Ruth was going to go and keep Beth company that night and she was taking Maggie.

"How's Maggie coping with all this? I mean, these two go back a long way." They were both looking at each other, concerned.

"She's devastated, wants to know what she can do, she wanted to come here today but Ruth said she would be better being with Beth tonight," said Jack.

"Yes, probably a good idea."

They both looked at each other and realised that their group was setting off, so ran up the carpark to meet them.

Chapter 9

Amanda was gowned up and ready for the operation, she had had all the checks and Nurse Suzie had been brilliant over the last three days, Amanda and Suzie were best of friends, and Amanda had been having more ice-cream. It was about the only food she could keep down.

Amanda had had the MRI scan and the neurologist, Dr Subramanian had come to go through the results. He stood there with his registrar, Dr Booth, looking at the notes, the scan results and the blood tests. They were in the family room just off the ward.

It had toys and colouring books, loads of crayons and a coffee machine. Beth looked at the poster of Shrek on the wall. They had loved that film. She placed her cup of water on the old coffee table.

"Good morning," said Dr Subramanian. "Now then, as you know we have found a mass on Amanda's brain, we will have to have a look at it, and that is why we are having this operation today. Once we're in and can see the tumour, we can decide where we go with the tumour. Do you understand so far? Do you want to ask any questions?" Dr Subramanian asked, looking at Ruth and Aaron.

Aaron nodded. "So you say, when you go in, can you explain the procedure?"

"Yes, no problem. Firstly, Amanda is put into a lovely sleep where she is monitored all the time she is under. Then, electrodes are fixed to different parts of her skull and body, this makes sure that when we are in there and we take the tumour out, we don't get too close to any nerves near the tumour and we don't damage them, it also means that we only cut out tumour and not living brain cells."

"What happens if you do?" Beth was looking concerned.

"There is a possibility of paralysis, or a stroke but that's not going to happen because we have these electrodes all over her brain, it tells us if we are close and stops us going any further. Then we cut a bit of the skull over the area of the tumour, and very carefully examine the tumour, cut a sliver off, this is called a biopsy."

"We send it to the lab, who, in about an hour, will tell us if it's cancerous or not, and while this is happening, we will have a discussion on what to do next. Now, in children, there is a good success rate that the tumour will be benign and, to tell you the truth, we will know with some certainty if it is."

"We usually start taking the tumour straight away and then send the rest to the lab. If everything is OK, we close and deliver her back to you, fit and well, a little bit groggy, but that's to be expected, she's just had a major operation. She will have all sorts of wires and tubes coming out and going in, but don't worry about them, they are there to check everything is working and to keep her stable."

"We'll take her to the neurology critical care unit, she'll be in there for 24 hours. After that, hopefully she is feeling better and she can go on to the children's ward and be home with you in about four to seven days."

Dr Subramanian looked at both of them.

"Does that answer all your questions?"

"Yes thanks, I know we are leaving Amanda in good hands, and I am sure you will do all you can. Thanks again, Doctor." Aaron was holding Beth's hand.

"Now, I've told you about the risks, do you want me to go over them again?" Said Dr Subramanian.

"No Doctor, we understand what can happen, and we also know that this is the best thing for our daughter."

Aaron turned to Beth and cuddled her really tightly.

Beth, pulling away, said to Aaron, "Look, it's going to work, she's our little baby and she's a fighter, just like her dad."

Aaron and Ruth shook hands with the doctors and walked to the children's ward to find Amanda. She was laid down on her bed, she looked really peaceful, like she hadn't got a care in the world, but that was all down to Nurse Suzie. She would be getting a big box of chocolates when they took Amanda home. She deserved it.

"Right," said Suzie, "the nurses from theatre are here, they will take you on a little ride to see the big doctor that's going to make you all better." Suzie smiled at Amanda, trying to put her at ease.

Amanda looked frightened and on the brink of tears. "You are coming with me, aren't you, Nurse Suzie?"

Suzie took her in her arms and smiled again. "Of course, my little fighter, I wouldn't leave you here on your own. Now, I'm sure you want Mummy and Daddy to come too." Suzie turned to see both smiling at Amanda.

"Of course, I don't go anywhere without them, I love them."

"I should hope you do, Miss Amanda."

Suzie came to the bottom of the bed and started pulling it from the wall and the other two nurses went to the top, and they went down the corridor to the theatre.

It was like a procession, with the bed in front of everyone, with Suzie walking at the side, watching Amanda, the other nurses at the top pushing and Aaron and Beth following close behind. Amanda seemed to enjoy the ride and jokingly said, "Are we there yet?" which got a response of laughter from everyone. Two doors opened on the left and Amanda arrived for her anaesthetic. This was the time they were all dreading.

Aaron and Beth kissed and hugged Amanda, said, "See you soon," and watched her fall asleep. She looked just like a baby, thought Beth and that was it, she broke, and the tears came flowing down.

Chapter 10

Matt was in the Branksome Arms on Poole Road. He'd seen Aaron going up to the retail park and he thought he knew the other fella, thought he met him when Aaron and Beth had a barbecue last month, but he couldn't remember his name.

He was sitting at one of the windows and could clearly see down the road to the mini roundabout at the bottom that helped traffic get from Ashley Road to Bournemouth Road, if you were going the other way, you get to Westbourne where he lived, then onto Bournemouth.

He had been there about an hour and was on his third pint. He was thinking about yesterday and the secret he had kept from Amanda. If she found out, it would be curtains for them both and a few others. He had every intention of helping to look for Amanda, and had been up to have a look earlier.

There was police, and search and rescue and a few gazebos. He didn't think it was ready yet, so that was why he was in the Branksome, having a drink, it was just down the road.

"Matt, Matt. For God's sake mate, are you deaf, MATT!" the guy shouted.

Matt jumped and looked at who was shouting, he recognised Ben and wondered why he was there. "Hi Ben, to what do I owe the pleasure?" looking at Ben, confused. "Can I get you a pint?" asked Matt.

Ben looked angry, and reminded Matt about that money he owed him. "Go on then, I'll have that pint, we can talk about the money when you get back."

Ben gave Matt a little smile and a wink. Matt had met Ben at a mate's 18th birthday party about six months ago. It had been a good night and they had got on well. Ben had liked Amanda, who had come with Matt for the ride, as Matt had put it. Ben not realising that they were an item.

Ben was a looker, in his twenties, broadly built, dark hair, and about 6ft tall, as Matt thought to himself, not someone he'd like to meet in a dark alley at night. The party was starting to wind down, so Ben suggested that they carry the party on at his place, and both Amanda and Matt who were a bit worse for wear, stared at each other, Matt saying, "Your mum and dad think you're at a sleepover at Maggie's, don't they?"

Amanda hunched herself up, looking at them both and in a drunken slur, said, "Yes, why, what's happening?"

Ben said, "You're coming to my place, we're carrying this party on, if it's alright with you, Amanda? I'd like you both to come."

Matt thought great, so they got their stuff together, said goodbye to the birthday boy, and got a taxi to Ben's house. They arrived at Poole Quay and entered the building through a pair of double doors. Ben had a swipe card, and in they went.

When they got out of the lift, Ben walked right down the corridor and Matt and Amanda just followed, not really knowing where they were going, too drunk to realise. Ben got to his apartment, opened the door and walked in, saying, "In here you two, the party restarts here."

Matt and Amanda sobered up very quickly when they saw where they were. They looked out the vast expanse of windows to see Poole Harbour and the sea in front of them.

"Good God, Ben, is this your pad?" Matt just couldn't stop looking around.

Ben smiled. "Erm, yep, not bad, is it?"

Amanda said in shock, "Stop me from prying, Ben, but how the hell do you afford a place like this? Isn't this Quayside, it must have cost you a fortune?"

"It did, or does, I rent it, fully furnished, £2000 a month, not a bad deal I thought. See, he wanted £2250 a month, so I suggested if I pay six months in advance, would he accept two grand a month, and for some reason, he snapped my hand off."

He was looking at Amanda and Matt who stood there with their mouths open.

"Anyway, let's have those drinks, what you'd want, Amanda, gin and tonic, anything," as he walked to a panel in the wall, he pressed a button exposing an inbuilt bar.

Matt said, "I like that."

"Glad you do, it's part of the furniture, now what's your tipple?" Ben was asking them both. Amanda had a G and T and Matt had a bottle of Stella. Amanda and Matt went over and sat on what looked like a very expensive sofa, pure white Italian leather, thought Matt. Ben sat opposite on the armchair with his whisky and coke.

Matt wanted to know, so his next question was, "Ben, I know Amanda asked you before and you don't have to tell us but, how do you afford this place, what do you do for a living, I'm curious."

Ben looked a bit surprised at the question, but knew he would have to tell them something. "Well, you see, my father is a banker in London. Has a house on Sandbanks. I'm into property."

"How do you mean, what's the most expensive place you've sold, then?" Amanda asked.

Ben just smiled. "Over a million now."

"Fucking hell, Ben, no wonder you can afford a place like this." Matt was admiring the view again.

"Well, it does bring in the money, that's for sure." Ben smiled. "Same again?" as he got up and walked to the bar, to get another round of drinks.

"That's amazing, Ben, how long have you been in the property game?" Matt asked.

Ben replied, "Well, it all started about five years ago, I went to my father with this idea about buying and selling properties, starting off cheap and then building up, asked him for a loan, which he gladly gave me. He knew I would make it work, and the rest is history, as they say."

Ben and Matt had been talking for a good hour, Matt telling Ben how he'd met Amanda and how well they got on, how she'd got a great family and, according to Aaron, her dad, it was his job to look after her. "Which I do."

Ben looked at Matt and replied, "And so you should, she's a lovely girl."

Amanda had slowly been falling asleep and was now slumped across the arm of the sofa with her feet on Matt's legs.

Ben looked over and said, "Well, Amanda looks like she's out of it."

"Yep, she does a bit, well, I think that's my cue for us to go home. I'll ring for an Uber. I have a rough idea where we are, I tell him to pick us up outside The Nelson; that should be OK, don't you think?"

Ben said, "Yes that would be about right."

But he was looking at Matt strangely. Matt noticed, asking, "Is there something wrong, what's that look, are you alright?"

Ben stared at the floor and rubbed his hands together, then looked up at Matt with a searching face. "What is it, Ben?" Matt was getting concerned.

Ben just thought, *here we go, I've got to ask him.*

Ben turned to face Matt. "Matt, please take this the right way, because I do class you as a friend now, I'm going to tell you something and you cannot tell a living soul, even Amanda. In-between all this buying and selling, I have a hobby and I'd like to bring you in on that hobby."

"What's that?" Matt now looked very confused.

Ben looked Matt right in the eyes and said, "Do you want to make some very good extra money, it's easy work, it'll take an hour out of your day every week and I can guarantee you £1000 for doing it."

Matt still looked confused, but after a while, it started to click. "I'm not doing that, selling drugs, you must be fucking mad, what the hell in the world made you think I would?" Matt looked at Ben in disbelief.

"Matt, you wouldn't be selling them, you would be taking a package from A to B, that's it, I've been doing it for two years now, I must have made just short of £80,000 in that time, just think what you could do with that amount of money. Think of what you could buy Amanda, think what you could buy for yourself, your family, it's easy money." Ben was trying to convince him.

Matt looked worried. "What if I get caught? What happens then? I've heard that it's a minimum of ten years for doing that."

Ben laughed. "Well, I've been doing it two years now and there hasn't been a sniff, you pick up at one carpark and drop off at another, you're never more than half an hour away and you just drive by and throw it in a bin at the other end, it's that easy." Ben was sitting there with his arms open.

"I don't know, Ben, it sounds OK, but I need to think about this, it's a big move and I've got to think of Amanda, I love that girl."

"Look Matt, I'm not going to pressure you in any way, just go away, think about it, think of the money you will get and what you can do with it. Give us your phone, I'll put my number in, ring me in a couple of days give and us your answer one way or another. There will be no hard feelings, OK?" Ben gave Matt an out.

***

Matt came back with the pint and put it on the table in front of Ben. "So, how's life treating you, still with that blonde with the amazing body?"

Matt tried to change the subject.

Ben was laughing. "Yes, why, have you been looking? Do you think you might get a piece of her? In your dreams, pal."

Ben looked at Matt with contempt.

"Where's my money? It's two and half grand, Matt, I'm not a bank, it wasn't a loan, you need to pay it and Mad Mick is shouting your name all over Poole, how much do you owe him. There is repercussion for not paying as I'm sure you know, they may have started, even now." Ben smiled a bit, then showed him the knife.

Matt sat back in shock. "What's that for?" Matt looked scared.

"It's called persuasion, I can't understand where all your money's gone, you must have had at least £20,000 over the last six months, where's it gone, Matt?"

Matt just put his hands in the air and said, "It's just gone."

Ben said, "I need my money by tomorrow, I'll see you back here at 2 pm, tomorrow don't forget, bring me the money and all will be good in the world." Matt was shitting himself.

***

The traffic was horrendous all around the retail park, people arriving all the time, but there was the added flow of the shoppers for the retail park itself. The police had cordoned off the lower part of the park where Decathlon was, they weren't too happy about that, but when they found out they could claim for any loss of business, they were a lot happier.

It was about 6:15 pm when Aaron and Jack came back to the command centre, Aaron felt knackered and Jack wasn't far off.

"Hey," said Rob to them both.

"You don't look so good, Aaron, are you OK?"

"Little bit tired, haven't slept for God knows how long, it seems like days. Any news?"

Aaron looked hopefully at Rob, but Rob's face told him the answer. "There are a lot of troupes still out there, we've had the ones from Bournemouth Road in, no luck I'm afraid, but there's still time tonight, there's another two hours of daylight, and we're back tomorrow." Rob was trying to lift Aaron's spirits.

"Aaron, I think it would be a good idea if you had a break now. I don't think you can do any more tonight, and your wives are back at home, I know you've been ringing her but I'm sure she'd like to see you now, and I imaging your son will be going crazy. I think it's a good idea, what do you say?"

Aaron was looking at Jack, and he just slumped down, saying, "You're right Rob, we'll come back in the morning, I need my bed."

"Good choice," said Rob.

"You're going to be no use to anybody, let alone Amanda, I'll see you both tomorrow, OK?"

Rob pointed in the direction of Aaron's house. Rob was saying the right thing, the pair of friends grabbed their kit. They had still had no sightings of Amanda. What would they tell their wives?

Chapter 11

April Smith, the liaison officer, was on her phone. Luke was sitting at the top of the stairs just outside Amanda's bedroom and was trying to get every last word of what was being said. April didn't know he was there.

"So, what you are saying is not to give them too much hope."

April's back was towards Luke, he shoved his hand to his mouth to stop the scream he was about to do. His face went red and he was breathing quickly.

"Yes, I will tell them that. How's the search going?" There was a pause. "That's good, any witnesses come forward?" Another pause. "That's even better. Look, I have to go now, Aaron and Jack are coming up the drive. I'll ask how it went for them, get a feel of how they are, tell them what's going on. OK, Glen thanks for that." And she ended the call.

Luke had managed to creep into his bedroom and was trying to cry quietly, he couldn't believe what he had just heard, there was no hope according to April, what was she talking about?

Aaron walked in first, followed by Jack, they both looked spent, but Beth and Ruth wanted to know every detail. Aaron just looked at them both and said, "Let us sit down first, is there any chance of a coffee? We're parched. I'll go through everything I know then."

Beth looked angrily at Aaron, saying, "That's alright for you to say, sit down, have a coffee, but you haven't been sitting here for hours, not knowing what the hell's been going on, it's murder."

Ruth put her arm round Beth's shoulders and looked up at Jack. Jack could see there was tension and knew there would be, so tried to calm it down.

"Look, we're all tired, and for good reason, you two haven't slept for the last day and a half, I can't imagine what you're going through. If this was Maggie, I'd be a bubbling wreck. We need to calm down, we need to be there for each other, we can get through this. Beth, you can get through this, you are the strongest women I know. Just don't give up."

April had heard all this commotion in the hallway and had gone into the kitchen and arrived in the lounge with a tray with a coffee pot and four mugs.

"Now then, I heard someone wanted a coffee." April, holding the tray and looking at them all.

Beth got up from the sofa and walked to Aaron and cuddled him tightly, saying, "Sorry, Jack's right, we need to stick together, that's the only way we're going to get through this." Beth paused and looked up, saying, "But I still want to know why this is happening to us, to Amanda, what have we done to deserve this, who wants to hurt us so much? It's killing me."

Beth, sobbing, slumped onto the sofa followed by Aaron, both of them arm in arm, consoling themselves. April realised she had to intervene and put the coffee tray on the table. April was now looking at all of them. "I've just come off the phone, Glen has just given me an update on what we know so far."

Aaron looked apprehensive and looked at Beth, saying, "Go on then, what do you know, and please tell us the truth, no pussyfooting around, I think we can take it."

April started by telling them about the search, that there were about 200 people out there now looking for Amanda, there were police dogs, Dorset Search and Rescue, who were co-ordinating the search because they were the experts in this field. She was sure that soon there would be a breakthrough.

Ruth looked up at April, saying, "But it's getting dark now, what happens then, do they stop looking?"

"No," said April. "They will carry on through the night, they have very strong spotlights that can light very large areas, they are designed to do this. We also have a witness who saw Amanda yesterday around 1 pm walking along Poole Road near Tesco's. We are waiting for the CCTV footage to come in later tonight, that's going to help us a great deal."

Aaron thought a minute and stated the obvious, "She left here at 11 am and was seen at 1 pm walking on Poole Road, it doesn't take that long to get to Tesco's from our house. Where was she for those two hours?"

April just said, "That's what we need to find out, and find out we will, we're on it, I promise you."

Beth was in a daze, but asked, "So that's it, that's all you've got."

"Look," said April, "I have been involved in many missing persons cases and I promise you that at the start, and don't forget, there are lots of things happening behind the scenes that are going on to get Amanda home. You just have to trust us, we do know what we are doing."

All of a sudden, the door slammed open, Luke rushed in, shouting at April, "You are lying, lying, I heard you on the phone."

Aaron got hold of Luke, who was crying his heart out. "What are you saying, Luke? What's wrong?" Bending down to look into his face.

Luke looked at April with a vicious look. "You said, not to give them too much hope," sobbing in-between words. "You're lying, why?"

"What do you mean, Luke?" Aaron was trying to calm Luke down.

"April was on her phone in the hall, I was outside Amanda's room just looking in, wondering where she was, I heard April say, not to give them too much hope."

"Luke, Luke, you've got it all wrong," April was trying to explain, "I was talking about another case I'm involved in, there was another girl who went missing last year, it was in Blandford, don't you remember, Aaron? She was found a few days later, it was all over the news."

"I was talking to Glen, he's a detective who's on the case with me because I was the liaison officer on that case too. The parent had got in contact, asked if we had arrested anyone yet, and DI Hudson had said we do have a few leads and are looking into them but nothing had come of our investigation and could I go and see them and tell them, but not to give them too much hope, it's ongoing."

"I'm sorry if you took my conversation the wrong way Luke, I told you all, I would never lie and I mean it, I hope that explains what you heard, Luke."

Luke looked at his dad who looked exhausted from it all and said, "There you go, Luke that's all it was, it's nice that you are concerned, and I know you think you may be being left out and that's our fault, it's not going to happen again, you are just as important to us as us getting Amanda back, so if you want to help, just ask, if you want to know anything, just ask, and we will tell you, OK."

"Love you, Dad," said Luke.

"What about your mum?"

Luke looked at his mum and smiled. "Mum knows I love her, I tell her all the time."

Chapter 12

Walters and Hudson were sitting in front of a computer screen, with Detective Glen Bishop standing behind, he had just loaded and brought up the surveillance tapes from Andrew Berlinski, the Tesco's manager.

Walters said to Glen, "We need to see between noon and 2 pm on the Sunday, that's when Cyril Parks said he saw her."

Bishop got the tape to midday and all three watched with interest. They had a good view of the whole carpark but it only showed two feet of the pavement in front of the wall, so when they looked at people on the pavement, those closest to the wall could be seen, but further into the road, you couldn't see their heads.

"Shit!" said Hudson. "We can't see them all in full, that's just great, all this time of waiting and it's going to be of no help."

Walters just turned and looked at her in disgust. "For God's sake, Sally, you haven't even given it five minutes, just let's have a look and see what comes up, OK."

It got to about 12:55 pm when, in the distance, a young girl came into focus. "Is it Amanda?" Glen shouted out.

"There, I see her, she's behind the guy on the mobility scooter. Zoom in, look she's got those frilly socks and white trainers, that's the first thing I saw, then the blond hair."

"Yes," said Walters.

"Good find, now let's watch what she does from here."

They watched closely as Amanda walked up the street, looking like she hadn't a care in the world. She was on her phone and wasn't watching what was happening in front of her; all of a sudden, a mobility scooter had to stop, as someone walked in front of it.

Amanda collided with the scooter. You could see she had hurt her leg because there was blood on her shin and she was hopping around on one leg. A woman came up and put her arm around her to steady her and you could see another couple of people around her. She looked to be telling them that she was OK, when Cyril Parks came into view.

"What's he doing there?"

Hudson was looking a bit shocked. "He didn't tell us about this happening, why, what's he hiding?"

Walters agreed, "I don't know but I think we need to have another chat with Cyril. Glen see if he's got a record, I'm curious."

They watched the rest of the video and saw Cyril comforting Amanda and pointing to Tesco's main entrance, you could see she was saying she was OK, and went to the mobility scooter driver to tell him the same, and just walked out of shot up Poole Road, with Cyril watching her go.

Walters turned to talk to them all, "Tomorrow is Monday, sorry it already is, this is what is going to happen. Glen, you get anything you can on Cyril Parks, Sally, check if Parks is working today, if he isn't, he gave us his home address, go and pick him up and bring him in, do it early, it might confuse him."

"I'm going to see the family, see how they're doing, we still need to find out what she was doing for that nearly two hours from 11 am to 12:55 pm. It's still a mystery. We need to fill in that timeline. Right, you all know what to do, go home, get a few hours' sleep and I'll see you sometime later, anything comes in, I want to know, night or day."

Chapter 13

Amanda woke up with a start, feeling that there was someone standing over her. She heard a voice in the distance, "Wake up. Wake up, you bitch, it's time to eat," said the voice.

She opened her eyes, feeling groggy, hoping it was still a dream and she would be in her bedroom, all warm and cosy in her bed, hearing the rest of the family getting on with their day. Luke not getting ready for school, Mum shouting up, "You're going to be late, if you don't hurry up, now come on."

Then Mum and Dad talking about some bill that needed paying and what they were paying and what they were doing at the weekend. Then all of a sudden, she realised she had all her clothes on, thank God for that. It was just a dream. No! It was a nightmare, and she didn't want that again.

"Amanda, get your arse into gear, I've brought you some food and coffee," the voice said again.

She could still feel the ties around her wrist but there seemed to be movement in her legs. Looking down, she realised that one of her legs was free but the other had a clamp around it and a chain coming from a loop which was secured to a post nearby. She only had one trainer on.

This was the first time in what she thought must have been a couple of days where she felt anything like human, if you can feel like a human Her hands were tied and chained to a post. She sat up and straight away felt dizzy, immediately falling back.

"For God's sake, girl," said the voice, "don't you want your food? I'm gonna leave it right here, next to your head."

She tried again, and as she got up, saw a dark figure standing at her feet, he had white trainers on. *Nike*, she thought, and then thought, if he wanted to disguise himself, why wear white trainers? As she looked further up, her heart started pumping fast, he was wearing a black balaclava with just two eye holes. She jumped, he just laughed.

"Scared you a bit, good because I have to tell you, I'm not a very nice man, well that's what my friends' tell me, and they are always right."

Amanda looked even more terrified, and starting breathing deeply and fast. "What do you want?" Amanda said very quietly.

The voice just looked and laughed a bit louder, saying, "Do you know, I haven't decided yet, my boss has left it up to me, he likes doing that. He has the last few times anyway."

Amanda was near to tears now and choked out, "What do you mean?"

The voice just looked her in the eyes and said, "That's for me to know, and for you to find out. Right, I've brought you some food and drink, I'm off now, see what the Crack is, I'll see you soon."

"What have I done? Why am I here? I want to go home. My parents will be wondering where I am," Amanda whimpered.

Just then Amanda saw her moment, the voice was looking the other way, she pulled all her strength together and sprang up and tried to get to the door, but the chain stopped her, it was only about four feet long.

"Nice try, darling. Don't you think I would have prepared for that? Stupid bitch."

He got up, moved the food closer to her, walked to the door and went outside. As he did, the room filled with light and Amanda couldn't see a thing. She tried to see where she was but there was no chance. The next thing she heard were locks and bolts going in, and at that moment, she knew she was going to die.

***

Matt had been trying to get the money for Ben. He was panicking now, he'd tried everyone he knew, but no one could help him. Ben had asked where his money had gone, Matt couldn't tell him he'd started gambling. For fuck's sake! He'd lost thousands. It started when he got his first thousand-pound payment.

It had gone brilliantly, Ben told him someone would be in contact after Matt told him he would give it a try, and, sure enough, a couple of days went by and someone did. He didn't know what to expect, it was short and sweet, he asked if that was Matt and Matt said, "Yes."

The man then just reeled off instructions, "A guy in a black Mercedes will be parked up near the bridge at Poole railway station carpark in an hour," the phone went dead. Matt laughed to himself, thinking that it was a bit cloak and dagger, but at least he knew where to go.

As he drove in, there were only about a dozen cars, so he saw the car more or less straight away. He drove round and pulled up next to them. The windows were blacked out, so he couldn't see much inside, but from their silhouettes, he could see two blokes sat in the front and one in the back.

They were big and all looked like hard nuts. The back window opened, a hand came out with a bag, Matt presumed it was his package. He took it and dropped it in the front door well. The man in the back told him, that the instruction was inside the bag, then the window closed and they drove off, leaving him in the carpark at 1pm with God knows what, presumably drugs and instructions.

Matt decided to drive off just in case someone was looking, a stupid thing to think really, there was no one around, well not that he could see. He came out of the carpark, followed the roundabout and stopped under the bridge. Leaning over, he grabbed the bag.

It was small, brown leather with red handles, it wasn't heavy. Opening it up, he saw what looked like small bags of drugs, they were tightly packed in a white cloth and taped with what he thought was parcel tape.

So that's what a brick of drugs looks like in real life, he thought. He felt the shape, sniffed at them, couldn't smell a thing, He saw a piece of paper in the bottom of the bag, pulled it out and found out what he was to do next. He was to drive to Bournemouth railway station, go to the back entrance, where there was a bin next to the car hire company, drop it in the bin and leave.

He thought to himself, *why couldn't they have dropped it off there themselves, it's not far.* They were testing him, that's what they were doing and he was right because over the next four months, he was making a drop nearly every week, picking up from Poole railway station and delivering packages all over Dorset. It was money for old rope.

As time went by, he started to enjoy his little outings and of course, the money came in very handy, in fact there was too much and he had to get rid of it, so he gave a bit to Amanda, telling her he'd won it on a bet at Poole Speedway. She didn't ask any questions and enjoyed spending it.

As time went by, he started from that one win to having a few more and found that no matter where he put the money, he couldn't get rid of it. He'd bought a new car and a nice watch, Amanda was still loving spending it.

Then, all of a sudden, his luck changed from winning to losing, it didn't happen overnight but he was losing more than he was winning. He had got a lot of his tips from the track where he had over time engaged in deals for a good tip, it was extra money, or so he thought.

They weren't working and every time he lost, he put more bets on to try and get the money he had lost back. It was a visions circle, and he couldn't get out of it.

He woke up one morning to find it had all gone. How? He thought he'd got this all under control, hadn't he? Seems not. He had to borrow some money, about two grand, but that was only to pay the other debts he owed. He finally went to Ben and asked him if he could borrow some money. He said he would go on the next two runs for free and would pay him back that way.

Ben had no problems with that arrangement, the problem was, Matt didn't keep up with his side of the deal. He kept coming up with all sorts of excuses, and the people Ben knew were getting annoyed with Ben and with Matt.

***

That's why, when Ben came into the Branksome Arms and threatened him, saying he needed the money back and then showed Matt his knife, Matt was shitting himself. He had to come up with a plan, somehow, he had to get the money.

He sat there for a couple of hours, thinking of every conceivable way he could get this money for Ben. Then something started ticking in his brain that looked and sounded perfect. But would it work? There was only one way to find out and that was to go ahead and do it.

Chapter 14

Hudson found out from Tesco's that Cyril was working that morning. She arrived there about 9 o'clock but couldn't see Parks anywhere. She drove into the carpark and parked near the doors in the parent and baby's bay, getting a few looks from the other customers.

Hudson ignored them all and walked into the store. She stood behind the two customers waiting to be served and quickly got to the desk, showing her badge, and asked if Cyril Parks had turned up for work that morning.

The assistant looked at the computer for staff sign-ins and said that he was. "Do you want me to put a shout out for him?" said the assistant.

"That would be great, thanks."

Hudson had to wait about ten minutes and saw Cyril walking towards her. Cyril was looking a bit confused, smiling, he said to Hudson, "Hello again, I haven't remembered anything extra from seeing that girl yesterday, has she been found? I hope so."

"No," answered Hudson. "We just need to verify some of the things you said happened."

Cyril looked confused. "Well, I don't know anything more to help you."

Hudson smiled at him. "It's alright, Cyril, it won't take more than an hour. If you can come down to the station, that would help us a lot, and I'm sure you would want to help, you're that sort of person, I can see it in your face."

"I'll have to square it with Mr Berlinski first, if that's alright with you?" He looked at the assistant, saying, "Julie, would you mind calling Mr Berlinski to the customer desk, I need to go to the police station to help with finding that girl who went missing yesterday."

Mr Berlinski came and was told what was happening. He looked at them both, saying, "I have no objection at all. Cyril, you just take the rest of the day off, I'll sort your rota out, you can make your hours up later in the week, is that OK?"

"Thanks for that, I do need the money, I can't lose a day's pay." Looking at DI Hudson.

Hudson saying to Cyril, "It's not going to take that long, Cyril, I promise you." Knowing full well it was going to take as long as it took.

"I'll need to go and sort my locker out and sign out, if that's OK?" Cyril was looking at Hudson.

"No problem. I'll wait here until you come back, my car's outside. We can go to the station in that. Don't worry, I'll bring you back."

Cyril walked away to the locker room to sort his things out, saying, "It should only take about five minutes and I'll be back."

"Thanks for that, Cyril, I'll see you in five."

Hudson and Mr Berlinski were both looking at their watches; it was taking longer than they both thought.

Hudson asked, "How do I get to the locker room?"

Berlinski showed her the way but when they got there, there was no Cyril.

Berlinski asked a store man, "Have you seen Cyril in here, Mark?"

Mark turned around and said, "Yes, he was here ten minutes ago, he looked to be sorting his backpack out, and he left through the delivery doors. Why, is there a problem?"

Hudson looked at Berlinski and said, "Oh yes, there is." She ran outside, made her way to the front of the supermarket, to see Cyril tearing up Poole Road towards Westbourne in his car.

Chapter 15

DI Walters had decided after he had been to see the family, he was going to go to Westbourne, to talk to the boyfriend. He had to persuade him to come down to the station.

The doorbell rang, Matt had been asleep maybe two hours, he just turned over and fell asleep again, the doorbell went again but for a lot longer this time. He shouted, "Fuck off, I'm asleep."

Then there was a loud banging—it was Walters, determined to wake him up. DI Walters shouted through the letter box, "Matt Fisher, this is the police, can you come down and open the door please?"

Matt fell out of the bed and hit his head on the bedside table. "Shit that hurt." He was still sleepy as he went downstairs to open the door. Then he panicked. "What do they want?" He had a little hash in his wardrobe, he turned back, saying, "Wait a minute, I've just woken up, I need a pee."

He went straight to the wardrobe and got rid of the hash out of his back window. He opened the door to find DI Walters staring at him. "Hello Matt, you look as if you had a good night last night." Smiling.

"You could say that," Matt replied. "How can I help you?"

Walters was smiling again, and said, "Oh, there's nothing to worry about, we just need to ask you a few questions about Amanda's disappearance. It can only help us find her. If you can come down to the station, any little detail you might know will only help us."

Matt asked, "Do I have to come now, I've only had a couple of hours sleep? Can't I come down this afternoon?"

Walters said, "Look Matt, Amanda is out there somewhere, we don't know what's happened to her, and I would have thought you would be doing everything in your power to find her."

Matt said, "Let me get dressed, if it helps to find Amanda, I'm all in."

Chapter 16

Amanda was coming around from the anaesthetic and, as Dr Subramanian had said, Amanda was very groggy, she had tubes all over, all Beth knew was that they were keeping her well and hopefully safe. The monitors beeped all the time and when they went off, she thought a nurse would have come up to check, but she found out later when Amanda was on the ward and asked Nurse Suzie, she said that they were trained to know when there was a serious bleep as opposed to a non-serious bleep. They were used to it.

As time went by and Amanda started getting better, it was nice to see her talking and moving around, all good signs that the operation had worked, they were told.

They were on their second day, and Amanda had had an MRI scan to see if all the tumour was out, and they were waiting on Dr Subramanian's ward rounds to find out. Beth didn't think that the man slept, he was there at 6am, he was there at 9pm, they'd even seen him in the middle of the night, caring for a patient that'd taken a turn for the worse.

Beth knew his name was Dr Subramanian, but to Aaron and Beth, his nickname was Dr Superman. What he did for brain tumour patients was beyond the call of duty, but they were a little bit biased after what he did for Amanda.

There was quite a noise coming from the adult ward down the corridor. Beth asked Nurse Suzie, "What was that all about?"

She looked up from checking the monitors of a boy called James who wasn't having a good time at the moment. The operation had been a success, he'd had the tumour removed about three days ago, but he had been put into an induced coma because of complications, the doctors were thinking he might have had a stroke.

It had been hard to watch; all the family had been told was time is a good healer. They had put him in this coma to let his brain rest, and would try and wake him up tomorrow and see if there was any improvement. Beth had been talking to James' parents quite a lot. There were spaces for four children on the ward but there were only three, and one of the girls had been discharged earlier.

That was amazing to watch, she had bounded down the corridor as if she was in a marathon, her parents trying to catch up and slow her down, falling was not a good thing to happen, not after major brain surgery.

Beth had told Mandy and Will, James' parents, that if they needed to talk or shout at anybody, she was their sounding board, and Aaron was, "Even better, I love being shouted at, I do it all the time, I'm experienced."

Mandy laughed, and said, "Yep, I've got one of them at home too."

They talked about their kids, how it all started and what the last two weeks had been like. Mandy had said, "It was as if I'd gone into a coma, I couldn't cope, if it hadn't been for Will, I don't know where I would have been. The worst thing about this is you feel helpless, there's nothing you can do."

Beth looked at Mandy and said, "Well, let me tell you something, you wouldn't have noticed, you both look as if you've got this covered."

"I suppose we have, in our own little way, but if the unspeakable happens— no, I don't want to even go there." Mandy started to well up.

"I hope you don't mind, Mandy, but I want to give you a hug."

"I think we both need a hug."

Mandy opened her arms and they embraced and held each other tightly. It was a good feeling, two souls in union.

Just then, a parade of doctors, registrars and nurses came marching in, pushing trolleys of notes and what looked like scans and X-Ray results, Dr Subramanian heading them all, they walked round to Amanda's bed and smiled, looking at her scans and her monitors. "Now then Amanda, I've been told that all you're eating is ice-cream, is that true?"

Dr Subramanian was looking over the top of the X-Rays. Amanda shyly looked at Nurse Suzie for help. "Can't help you there, Amanda, I'd been telling you that was enough ice-cream now, but I saw you persuading Nurse Boulton that the doctors had said that was the only food you could eat."

Beth said, "When did that happen?"

Nurse Boulton butted in and said, "It's a good job I knew she was trying to pull the wool over my eyes, you should have seen her face when I came back with some toast, she wasn't smiling then, sorry Amanda."

They all started laughing, Amanda just said, "That wasn't fair, I'm the one that's poorly."

Dr Subramanian stopped laughing and again started looking at all of Amanda's results, asking Amanda, "How are you feeling Amanda, have you got any pain, because if you have, we can sort that out."

Amanda said, "Just a little."

"Well Amanda, it looks like your operation was a success." Dr Subramanian turned to Aaron and Beth, smiling. "The tumour has all gone, the scan shows that the biopsy has come back negative, so everything is clear, so that's great news."

Aaron and Beth just fell into each other's arms and started sobbing, sobbing with relief, all they could say was, "Thank you. Thank you. Thank you."

Mandy and Will, who were sitting next to James, were smiling and putting thumbs up to them all. There was a bleep above James' bed. It was one of those serious bleeps that Nurse Suzie had talked about earlier. They all looked round. Dr Subramanian ran across the ward and noticed that James' heart had stopped. He immediately started doing CPR and told Nurse Suzie to get the crash trolley.

Nurse Boulton ran and pulled the curtains round the bed, and Mandy and Will were asked to stand outside while the doctors dealt with James. All anyone could hear were doctors calmly giving orders. Dr Subramanian then asked for adrenaline, all the time the bleep carried on like a smoke alarm going off, occasionally bleeping rapidly then stopping again.

Another doctor was getting some Atropine ready at the request of Dr Subramanian. The Atropine was given and it seemed to be working, James was still in his induced coma but it seemed his heart was coming round. Then nothing, it stopped, there was also no brain activity on the monitor, all the doctors looked at the monitors, looked at each other and all Mandy heard was Dr Subramanian saying, "Is everyone in agreement, that we call this one?"

Mandy screamed and fell to the floor. The whole ward went quiet, knowing what had happened and thanking God it wasn't happening to them.

Chapter 17

Another night had gone by, and Amanda had tried to come up with any explanation as to why this was happening to her. She remembered walking up Poole Road and falling, wait a minute, she seemed to remember a mobility scooter, and bumping into it, and then it was a blur.

She wished she could remember more. Her wrists were hurting, the cable ties were cutting into them, there was dried blood all up her arms and all over her white t-shirt, which must have happened when she tried to escape. Mum was going to kill her, look at the state of her t-shirt.

The man's voice came back to her again, she thought she recognised it, but couldn't put a name to it. She was getting angry with herself. She was a fighter, why was she thinking so negatively?

Daybreak had just arrived and it was lighting a little area in her cage, as she put it. She could see a pitchfork, a hand shovel and some rope. It was some sort of shed, maybe a lean to, she sat there for a while and concocted a plan of action to escape again.

She knew from the last try that the chain length allowed her to get about half a metre from the door, it was a mad idea but if she could get there with the pitchfork and the hand shovel, she might be able to dig under the door and scurry out, there was only one thing stopping her. The chain was attached to her ankle, she had to get that off somehow, but how?

She was looking around when she noticed she hadn't eaten the food the voice had left her. She wasn't hungry. She recalled it had been an egg mayonnaise sandwich and she was allergic to eggs. Stupid man! Now, the clamp was quite loose, she had a small ankle and had thought with a little persuasion and egg mayonnaise, she might be able to squeeze her ankle out.

She opened the sandwich and scooped out the filling, and butter, and put it all into her hand and then proceeded to smother the gunk all around her little ankle.

Carefully, she tugged at the brace and it started to slip over her ankle, it was a tight squeeze at the heel but she persevered, slowly and surely it started to come off, then bang, it dropped to the floor, dust and mud dispersing all around the room.

"Yes," she cried, and proceeded to run to the door, falling over straight away, forgetting she'd been tied up for more than three days and her legs were weak.

"Crawl," she told herself, and did eventually get to the door. She brought the pitchfork up and thrust it into the ground, and it went straight in. There was a cry of joy, she carried on until there was a channel, she thought she could slide through. She listened to make sure the coast was clear.

She got her shoulders through, and half her back and was overjoyed with her progress when she felt this enormous pain in the middle of her back, it was like someone had stomped down on her hard. She screamed and tried to scramble back but the pressure got even harder.

"Where do you think you're going to, my little mole?"

The voice had returned and he was not too pleased. The next thing Amanda felt was a kick to the side of her ribs. She screamed even louder and was trying to get her breath back. She tried to move but her whole body was in a spasm, not good, not good at all.

There was a lot of noise as bolts were being unlocked and chains being pulled, then another bang as the door swung open and Amanda felt herself being dragged to the centre of the room and sat down with her back to the post and tied extremely tightly to the post with the rope that was on the floor.

She screamed in pain, all the time this was happening, and shouted at him, "You fucking bastard, you child beater, I know you're going to kill me, so why don't you do it now? Put me out of my misery."

He was silent for ages then he leaned down, right next to her ear, and very quietly said, "I will kill you when I think it is right to do so, and not until. You are worth more alive than dead."

Again, another long pause before he said, "We'll both have to wait patiently, to see what the outcome is." Then he shouted in her ear, "Don't you ever try that again, or you will be meeting your maker very soon, understand?"

Amanda shook her head, not saying a word, just looking up at this man still wearing his balaclava, trying to recognise the voice, she was sure she knew but it wasn't coming to her right now. But she was sure it would. Then she heard the bolts and chains being closed again and thought to herself, *if I'm going to die, I'm going to die fighting, you just wait and see, bastard.*

***

DI Walters was sitting in his office in the Detectives' Room. There must have been at least twenty officers, either on the phone or checking leads from the helpline, Crime-stoppers or people who had just walked in with information about Amanda and what they knew or what they'd seen.

DS Hudson was standing outside the back of the station in the carpark, knowing that DI Walters was going to bollock her for what had happened with Cyril Parks. But to her, it wasn't her fault and that was what she was going to tell him. She arrived on the second floor after taking the steps, passing colleagues who were saying, "Good luck, Sally, you're going to need it."

She asked, "Is he on the war path?" looking at Glen.

"Oh my God, Sally, all he can say out loud, mind you, are, what the fuck was she doing, having a cup of tea with the manager while he saunters out of the back? What a dipstick."

"Thanks for the heads up, Glen," she said, as she proceeded to walk into the office. It went very quiet, and it felt like all eyes were on her, and they were.

All she heard next was Walters' voice saying, "Hudson, my office, now." Walters walked to his office, which was all the way at the bottom of the main office, so she had to walk the corridor of shame, past all her other work mates, who started taking a sharp intake of breath as she walked past.

Hudson replied under her breath, "Piss off."

Walters was standing behind his desk when she went in and he told her to sit down, which she did. All he could do was stare at her, he'd try to start a sentence and then think better of it, you could see he was physically calming down because he finally said, "Go on then, I can't wait to hear what you're going to come up with for this cock-up."

Hudson just looked at him and thought, *do I tell him it wasn't my fault? No, I'd better not.* "Look Steven, I—"

Walters interrupted, "DI Walters to you."

"Sorry, look it happened so fast, I'd got him to agree to come down to the station to answer a few questions, he asked if he could change out of his work

77

clothes, told me they were in the locker room. I didn't see that as a problem, so let him go."

"Why had you gone to ask him to come down to the station?" Walters was searching for an answer.

"Because we'd seen him having a conversation with Amanda outside Tesco's and he hadn't told us about it."

"That's right, Hudson, don't you think Parks might have thought we might be onto him and he needed an excuse to disappear?" Walters was staring at Hudson.

"It never came into my equation, it does now, of course. I'm so sorry, DI Walters, it won't happen again."

"No, it won't, because if it does, you will be transferred to the countryside for your sins and that would mean, Goodbye and Good Riddance. Do you understand, DI Hudson?"

She nodded, turned and walked out of the room, thinking, *God, have I just got away with that?* Then, there was a loud shout that ate into the back of her neck, and Walters said, "Hudson, you've got 24 hours to find Parks or you're off the case. You made the mistake, now you go and solve it, got it?"

"Yes, Sir."

Hudson did not look back.

Chapter 18

It was about midnight and Beth had finally got Luke to bed. *Thank God for that*, thought Beth and walked into her bedroom to find Aaron sitting on the edge of their bed, looking at a family photo album, sadly. She looked at Aaron and thought that this was the first time they had been alone in the house together for nearly three days.

Everyone had gone, all her friends, Aaron's friends, Matt, even April, she had gone back to the station earlier to see if anything had come in and to touch base with the rest of the detectives. Beth stood at the doorway and watched Aaron turning the pages, he looked exhausted, sometimes smiling and sometimes, he'd give a little chuckle. Beth knew that album by heart, she'd looked at it so many times.

She smiled, saying, "I bet that's bringing back memories."

Aaron looked up and was surprised to see her there. "Hello love, I'd half expected you to be fast asleep with Luke."

Beth smiled. "No, I finally got him off and wondered where you were, I didn't think I would see you looking down memory lane."

"No, neither did I, I haven't looked at these for ages. It's amazing at what has to happen to make you think of it. Sorry, is it bothering you? I can put it back if you want me to." He looked apprehensively at Beth.

"No, it's nice, funnily enough, I had them out last week, I got the giggles as well, just looking at what we got up to, what the kids did and where we went."

Aaron pointed. "Look at this. There is you and Luke burying me in the sand, all that stuck out was my head, you were on my chest, but unbeknown to me, Luke and you had concocted a plan, and just before you took the photo, Luke put a crab on my face, I jumped out of my skin, I couldn't move."

"I'd got all that sand on me and you on my chest. I was trapped, and how funny you thought it was and so did everyone else around, but I did promise, I seem to recall when I was released and the crab scuttled down the beach sideways that I would get my revenge. I did, didn't I?"

"Oh my God, you did, we had to agree to stop after that, the kids were starting to do all sorts to each other and to us." Beth laughed gently.

"Do you know, I can't remember what happened." Aaron was looking all innocent.

"You know what you did." Beth looked at Aaron. "You got Amanda to go to the toilet and come back with some water, didn't you?" looking at Aaron with a wry smile.

"I didn't know the barman was going to give her a whole jug," smiled Aaron.

"No, you could have stopped yourself there, but you chose not to, didn't you? I wondered where you'd gone, you were ages, I looked at Amanda and asked if she'd seen Daddy and Luke just started laughing as a jug of ice cold water was poured down the back of my lovely white dress."

"There was a big roar in the place, but to make it worse, I stood up quickly in shock and it just carried on down the rest of the dress and all over the front. I was drenched. The roars got louder and after a while, I had to admit and say touché. That was a good one."

Aaron looked so much happier, like his old self. "The best bit was watching you going back through the hotel as if you'd been to a wet t-shirt competition." Laughing even more. "Oh Beth, we had some magical times, didn't we?"

"Do you know," Beth said, "the best times are when we were on a bench in a park, watching them play on the swings, Amanda pushing her little brother, you shouting out, not too high, Amanda; them running over to the slide, taking it in turns to come down, then you going to have a go and getting stuck half way down, then Luke coming up to rescue you by coming behind you as fast as he can to push you to the bottom and you both landing in a heap on the ground. That's what I like to remember."

Aaron went quiet and then said, "What about Amanda, I look at this photo of her when she was, I don't know, maybe fourteen, she looked so grown up but so innocent with that amazing smile and I think bad things, I know I shouldn't, but it's hard not to. I don't think it's sunk in yet, but looking at these photos is helping."

"All I can say is, when you want to talk, whenever that is, just nod, kick me, say something and I will be all ears. I am here for you, whatever happens, I hope you know I love you so much and we can get through whatever life throws at us, so long as we do it together."

Beth just wrapped her arms around his neck and squeezed him tightly, kissing him on the neck, saying, "We will. We will."

They fell to the bed and started to kiss passionately, both saying they loved each other and crying. They held each other, knowing nothing was going to happen, it was a need they both wanted and a need they both wanted to give. They both fell asleep for the first time in days.

Chapter 19

Cyril had not gone home, he knew if he went there, he would get arrested. He'd given his address to that copper. Mind you, they could have got it from work, but he knew he hadn't done anything wrong, so why had he run? He didn't know. He'd answered all their questions, what more did they want?

He knew they would have looked to see if he had a criminal record; that was as read, so as sure as the Pope's a Catholic, they would have found out he'd molested a child when he was young, but that was 40 years ago.

He'd done his time and he'd been clean ever since. He knew he shouldn't have given his details, he just wanted to help that poor girl and their parents, He couldn't imagine how they were feeling.

He had to get away, he had to think. He saw his opportunity and took it, anyone would have done it. He needs to get out of Poole. He'd got a mate who lived in Boscombe, just outside Bournemouth. He'd known her for years. She would help him, he knew, she owed him a favour.

He thought she had a flat on Gladstone Road. He used to take her drugs there, that's why she owed him the favour. He was sure she would put him up for a few nights while this all blew over. He needed the next train from Bournemouth to Boscombe.

He was in Westbourne and so he would get a bus into Bournemouth, leaving his car at home, so the cops would think he was still at home, get a train from Bournemouth station to Pokes Down, the nearest station for Boscombe, and he would be there, easy.

He got to Bournemouth station and was walking through the back entrance where he was going to catch his train to Pokes Down, when he noticed a police presence.

"What the fuck are they doing here? It's only been about two hours, surely, they haven't put two and two together and made four, no way."

Anyway, he'd got no choice now, he'd keep a low profile, keep his head down, pay for his ticket on the train. Just then the announcement came over the Tannoy, "The train arriving on platform two is the Twelve-Thirty-Three to London Waterloo arriving at Fourteen-Twenty, stopping at Pokes Down, Brockenhurst, Southampton Central, Southampton Airport Parkway, Basingstoke, Woking, Clapham Junction and London Waterloo. First Class, is in Coach A, refreshments will be sold on board."

He then noticed that there was a group of coppers round the cafe, when one of them turned to look at him, he just froze. The copper started to walk towards him, Cyril was shitting himself. As he got up close, he bent down to get something out of his rucksack and the copper said, "Excuse me?"

He stood up and thought this was it.

"Can I just pass, I need the toilet?"

He hadn't realised he was standing right in front of the entrance, Cyril looked and said, "Sorry officer, didn't realise where I was," and moved to the side, smiling. "Bloody hell," he said under his breath as the copper went in.

He picked his rucksack up and walked to the train and got on, sat in an unreserved seat and waited for the train to leave, which it did minutes later. He looked out of the window and couldn't help but look at the parade of coppers doing their due diligence and making a complete cock-up of it, and a smile came to his face.

Chapter 20

It was 3 am and Matt was standing round the back of a chemist on Poole Road. His trade was drugs now, and his thoughts were, *if I get some of my own drugs, I can sell them and get the money that way.* It sounded a good plan, well, to him it did, he just had to get in.

He had his mask on and he'd brought a bag with some gloves, a knife, a hammer, some wire cutters and a screwdriver. He also had some cling film and a little torch. He had no idea what to do, he'd never broken into anywhere before, but needs must.

He'd looked on Google, firstly on how you might be able to break glass without it breaking into millions of pieces and landing all over the place, that's where the cling film came in. When he watched a video of it, thinking to himself, what a brilliant idea, it looks like it works, here's hoping.

He also googled how to stop an alarm from going off, and he was amazed that it showed him how to do that as well. He didn't know if Google thought they were helping the general public with a problem with their alarm in the house when it wouldn't stop, or helping the general public on how to remove broken glass safely from a window, a safe way to do DIY, but hey, THANK YOU Google, it was helping him with what he needed to do.

Opening the bag, and getting the torch out of his pocket, shone it into the bag and found the cling film. He'd thought ahead and brought cling film that was on a roll attached to a gripper, so he didn't have to find the end, he just had to pull and tear to the right length.

This he did, finding a window that was big enough for him to get through, and low enough not to have to struggle. Looking at the window with the cling film on it, got the hammer in his hand and thought, here we go. He went to hit the glass but hesitated, he chickened out, for God sake Matt, what are you playing at, just hit the bloody thing.

Starting to tap the glass, which was doing fuck all, in fact it was echoing all around. Shit, he thought, oh well, here we go and just hit it There was a dull sound, and the next thing he saw when he pulled his torch up to the window was a crack that went from one corner at the top to the other corner at the bottom, and where the hammer had hit was a crystallised circle about twelve inches in diameter, but it was all held together with the cling film.

He yelped, probably a bit too loud and quickly brought his arm up to muffle any more excitement. He sat there, looking at his handwork for a good five minutes, and then thought, phase two. He gently started pushing the glass and, yes, it moved forwards into the room, but the whole window didn't fall, the centre where the crystallised glass was had gone, and half the top of the window was gone, but it still left the other half of the window just sitting in the frame.

He looked in horror, he was just going to have to pull the glass out, and carefully. Putting his gloves on, he got hold of the biggest piece and started moving it backwards and forwards and eventually, it broke with a pinging noise. *Not too bad,* he thought.

Now for the little piece in the bottom left corner. He started doing the same but nothing was happening, it was stuck, that baby was going nowhere. Deciding to leave it, there was loads of room for him to get in. Going through and landed on a counter and then slipped to the floor. That was easy.

Dragging his bag through and put his torch on, he realised he was in the staff room. Watching where his torch was taking him, realising all of a sudden, he couldn't believe his luck, his torch was shining on the burglar alarm. He knew what to do, he'd watched it on Google and it seemed to work.

He found the fuse isolation box, took out the fuse that took the electric out, then he unscrewed the front panel of the main box and took the main motherboard out and unplugged it. There was nothing, no sound, no alarm. *Brilliant*, he thought, *now I need to be quick, I need the good stuff.*

He wasn't worried about CCTV, he had a mask on, he'd seen all those programmes on the TV and knew he had to wear black, no signs on his clothes, be invisible. This he was.

He walked round the shop and found the main cabinet that had the hard drugs in, it was in another room in the back. "Shit," he said to himself, it was locked. What did he expect? He got his screwdriver and hammer out of the bag and started on the lock. It opened quite easily.

He opened the doors and there they were; Xanax, Valium, Ratline, and Fentanyl. Thinking all his Christmases had come together, he was going to make a fortune. He opened his bag and swept his arm across the shelves and they all just fell into the bottom of the bag. He wasn't bothered what they were, all he knew was this was his lifeline.

In the distance, he could hear an alarm blaring out and his first thought was, where the hell was that coming from? Then all of a sudden, he realised it was coming from above him. *How the hell was that going off,* he thought, *when I get back home, I'm going to complain to Google, they got that bit wrong.*

Matt just panicked, picked the bag up and ran for the staff room, his torch in front finding the way. He arrived at the window and climbed on to the counter with ease, but he was rushing to get out and was trying to hold onto the torch, the bag and the window, and had forgotten the shard of glass that was still in the frame.

There was a sharp pain in his hand as the glass cut through the middle of his palm and broke. It was sticking out the other side. He just looked at his hand and the blood, and screamed, saying, "Well, I've just fucked that up big time."

He made his way back down between the buildings onto Poole Road and tried to walk as slowly as he could without looking suspicious, he had his hand in his pocket but all the time, leaving drops of blood in his wake.

***

Walters looked at Hudson. "What you mean you've lost him? HOW? I don't believe you, Hudson, I give you an easy task, I give you all the people you need, and he slips right past you. I'll ask again, how?"

Hudson looked at Walters for what seemed like a lifetime, the whole office was watching and waiting for her reply. Hudson started very quietly, "Boss," looking him straight in the eyes, "I had every avenue covered, his house, the bus station, the railway station."

"I had BOLO out for our patrols everywhere. I relied on the lot of them doing their jobs, but it seems the guys that were at the railway station were more bothered about food breaks and going for a piss. An officer asked a commuter if they had seen this man anywhere on the station, and she'd said she had seen him get on the train," Hudson was now getting a bit louder, "THAT WAS GOING

TO LONDON. Boss, there are at least eight stops on the way to London, he could have got off at any of them, he could be anywhere."

Walters realised that Hudson was not to blame and had tried to get everything covered. He looked at Hudson. "Right, we have to find him, and quickly. Ross and Moore, I want you to go to the station and find out where he bought a ticket to, then I want you to go down to that station and ask to look at their CCTV to see if he got off there and, if he did, can you follow him from there to where he might have gone?"

He looked at Hudson and said, "Now then, Sally, have you calmed down? I hope you have because we've got a job to do and I can't do it without you."

Hudson just looked up at Walters and said, "Aw, Boss, this sounds like a proposal."

Hudson and the rest of the office started laughing, Walters saying, "Come on then, I've got Matt Fisher in the interview room, let's see what he has to say."

Chapter 21

Luke was on the floor in front of the telly, playing one of his games. He had his headphones on, so he couldn't hear what was happening in the room, but boy, everybody in the room could hear Luke. There was shoo tie shoo tie, bang bang coming as a running commentary in Luke's voice, and pretty loud.

Aaron heard a knock at the door and went over to Luke to tell him to shut up, and pointed to the door. Luke ignored his dad and carried on. Aaron went to the door on the second knock, shouting, "Alright, alright, I'm on my way. Luke, turn that thing off."

Tapping him on the head. Luke looked up, saw his dad going to the door and paused the game. Aaron opened the door to find April, the liaison officer standing there with a smile on her face.

"Hi Aaron, have you got a minute?"

Aaron looked at her hopefully and thought they'd found her. "Tell me you've found her, is she alright? Where is she, can we go and see her?"

Beth heard all this, Aaron had left her in bed when he woke up, he'd looked over at Beth and, as she was in the land of nod, had left her to catch up on some sleep. The door opened and Beth started shaking again, looked at Aaron, then at April and managed to get out, "Have you got my baby?"

April said, "Can we sit down, I need to tell you where we are. I told you at the start, I'm here to keep you informed and that's what I'm doing."

Beth got even worse, started hyperventilating, "What do you mean, where we are, what the fuck are you doing to find my daughter?"

Aaron went across and tried to calm Beth down, Luke just stared at his mum, his eyes starting to water.

"Come on, let's sit down and we can all hear what's going on, we're all ears, April."

April wasn't looking forward to this, she knew it wasn't good, and there was no way she was going to paste over the truth. April looked at them all and started to say, "Look, we haven't found her yet, but that doesn't mean we don't have any clues or leads. We have her on video walking past the Tesco's on Poole Road, just before 2 on Sunday afternoon and it looks like she was on her way to Matt's. I gather he lives in Westbourne."

"Yes," said Beth. "So, she was still about at 2 on Sunday afternoon?" Beth was looking at April for answers.

"Yes, but after that we don't know, we are trawling the area for more CCTV be it from houses, doorbell security, buses. We're asking people house-to-house whether they saw anything that morning. We have a good lead already on that, and I promise you, it is being taken seriously."

Aaron sounded dejected, saying, "So is that it, that's all you've got, after over, what, two maybe three days, that's it?"

April looked at the floor, wondering whether to tell them about Matt. "We have to talk to everyone as I said in the beginning and we do have a few leads."

She paused for what seemed an age and came back to tell them, "We are talking to Matt at the moment, we're hoping he might be able to help us."

Beth said, "You don't think Matt had anything to do with this, do you?"

April replied, "No, he's just helping us with our enquires. We have to ask everyone who was close to Amanda. I'm sorry but we'll have to ask you what you know soon, you might be able to give us that little piece of something, no matter how small you think it might be, that can help us find Amanda. Can I ask, have you ever heard of Amanda taking drugs at all? I'm sorry, I have to ask."

Aaron shot out of the chair and looked at April, eyes wide open, and going red in the face, He shouted at April, "Don't you ever think that my daughter would ever think of doing drugs, she hated them, she's always coming in and saying so and so has taken this and so and so has taken that, she goes mad. So, I don't think she is a candidate for a drug user, do you?"

April put her hands up and said, "Aaron, I'm really sorry but I have to ask these questions. It's not nice asking them but I have to. Now since yesterday night, have you heard anything that might help us, anything? Like have you heard from any of her friends? Have any of your friends rung up with information? This is how we will find her, people talking, people remembering, it all helps."

They all looked at each other for inspiration but nothing was coming through. "Sorry," said Aaron, "I shouldn't have got so defensive, I know you are doing all you can. But it's hard to hear you asking if Amanda was taking drugs."

April just stood up and smiled at them all and said, "Look, I've told you where we are, and I know there will be more to come, just bear with us. In all my years of looking for missing people, there is one detail that makes us find someone, and it will happen for Amanda."

She said her goodbyes and said, "I will keep in touch."

***

Matt was sitting in the interview room, he'd been there for hours. Detectives kept coming in and offering coffee and a sandwich, and he'd say no to the sandwich but yes to the coffee.

"How long's this going to take? I've been here hours now, where's the guy who brought me in?" asked Matt.

The detective said, "Sorry mate, he's had to deal with another part of Amanda's disappearance. He knows you're here and sends his apologies, but hopes you understand, he'll be with you as soon as he can, I'm sure."

Hudson and Walters were actually sitting just opposite the interview room and had been there for a couple of hours going through all that they knew about Matt Fisher. They knew he lived in Westbourne in a flat over a carpet shop and had been there for about twelve months.

Before that, he had lived in a flat in Boscombe. He'd worked at Halford's at Pokes Down Hill, Detective Glen Bishop was looking into his work record and was to report back soon. His police record showed that apart from a pull for cannabis eighteen months ago in Boscombe, where he got a warning, there was nothing since. They'd heard through a source that he liked to gamble, and had a group of friends that he associated with. Nothing to really worry about.

"Right," said Hudson. "Are you going to lead or do you want me to?"

"You start," said Walters. "I'll just watch and listen."

They got up and both walked to the door of the interview room, Hudson knocked and walked in with a notepad and pen, Walters followed close behind.

"Hello, Matt, my name is DS Sally Hudson, and you've already met DI Steve Walters; how are you doing? Firstly, I have to apologise for the long wait, it has been mental out there. When someone goes missing, it's all hands to the wheel, as I'm sure you appreciate."

Matt just looked at them both and said, "That's OK, as I said to DI Walters earlier, anything I can do to help."

Hudson started by asking him, "How long have you known Amanda?"

"Oh, about nine months."

"Where did you meet?" asked Hudson.

"Well, it was really through a friend of Amanda's. I'd met Maggie first, at the Dolphin Centre, she was there with some friends, we were just talking, having a laugh, when Amanda came to join us. Do you know, I fancied her from the first moment I saw her."

"It was that long blond hair and she didn't look sixteen. She was more mature. I got to know her that afternoon. I plucked up the courage to ask her out, and the rest is history, as they say."

Hudson smiled, said, "I suppose it was love at first sight."

Matt smiled back, saying, "I suppose you could say that."

Hudson looked at Matt and asked, "How do you get on with Luke? I bet he can be a bit of a pain sometimes."

Matt looked confused. "How do you mean? We get on very well, always have done, from the first time we met. He can be a bit in your face sometimes but on the whole, he knows when he's not wanted, when Amanda and me need space."

"Oh well, that's good," said Hudson. "So, how often do you go into his bedroom when he's not there?" Matt again looked confused.

"What the hell are you on about?"

Hudson took a file from Walters and started reading a statement from Beth about the argument that Amanda and Luke had had on the morning of her disappearance. "She said it was something to do with you breaking his console, his pride and joy. What was that all about?"

Matt looked angry. "For God's sake, we'd been playing together the night before and I'd left something in his room, I can't remember what it was, his room is a mess. I didn't know that his console was lying on the floor and yes, I stood on it, but it wasn't my fault, as I explained to Amanda."

"So, where do you think Amanda is? The last we have of her is walking along Poole Road about 2 pm on Sunday, obviously coming to see you, had you arranged to meet her?" Hudson was looking at Matt for an answer.

"No, I hadn't. I'd told her the night before when she texted me, telling me she'd had a mighty row with her dad that I was going out with the lads, and I would see her later on the Sunday afternoon, so I don't know why she was coming to see me, she knew I wasn't there."

"OK," said Hudson. "That's about it for the moment, thanks for coming in, it's much appreciated, but we might need your help in the future, if that's OK with you?"

Matt smiled and said, "I've said it earlier, if it helps to get Amanda back, I'm in."

They all got up from their chairs and Walters went for the door. He looked at Matt and asked, "So, what have you done to your hand? It looks a bad cut, that's a lot of bandage."

Matt looked at his hand, then at Walters and said, "Oh that, I was doing some work at the flat and I cut myself on a glass door in a cabinet I was building in my bedroom. I dropped it, tried to catch it. I know, stupid, but it went right through my hand, that hurt a bit, but it's alright now."

"Didn't you go to A&E?" asked Walters.

"No, I stopped the bleeding and wrapped it up in a bandage, and it's fine."

Walters looked at Matt and said, "Keep an eye on that, don't want it going septic, do we? Anyway, thanks again for coming in, we'll talk again, I'm sure."

Walters opened the door and watched as Matt turned right and went down the stairs to the exit. Walters looked at Hudson and said, "He's lying, he hasn't told the whole truth. There's something fishy about him."

Hudson laughed. "Don't you think it could be something to do with his name?"

Walters looked at Hudson, thinking what the hell was she on about, then all of a sudden, it clicked. "For God's sake Hudson, grow up."

Hudson laughed again. "Well, I thought that was a good one, a hint of genius on my part. Oh well, what's next?"

"We just keep on looking, that's all."

And Walters walked into the office, leaving Hudson at the top of the stairs, wondering whether Steve was right.

Chapter 22

Rob Clark had returned to the search tents. It was about 8am and he was looking for his deputy, Kristy Scott, who had taken over the co-ordination of the search teams at about 2am. He was grateful that the tea tent was still in action, and the amount of people that were still there.

Rob looked at Kristy as he walked up, "Morning Kristy, how are you this morning? Any news? It's still looking busy."

Kristy looked up from her table and realised it was Rob and said, "Oh, hi Rob. Yeah, it's been hectic. Well, we may have had a breakthrough, one of the team was on Princess Street in the playground, thought it was an ideal place to look, and in one of the bushes, he found a trainer. It was white, Nike, and a size five. They knew it was one of the items that was on the description list as to what she was wearing, so rang through to me."

Brilliant, thought Rob. "Who's got the trainer now?"

"Well, I got the call about 6:30 this morning, and I informed the police. They were here within twenty minutes. A detective called Glen Bishop arrived, he said he was one of the detectives on the case. First thing he asked was, has anyone touched it. I said no, what do you think, we do know what we're doing?"

"Yeah, sorry. I didn't mean that, the play area is just off Princess Street, I gather, near the roundabout? I said yes. Right, I need to get forensics there, is your team still there? He said. Yes, they're guarding the trainer with their lives. Thanks for that, he said, got in his car and went." Kristy looked at Rob and said, "He needs to get his face from up his backside."

Rob laughed. "Now then, Kristy, we all have to get on together, we don't know how long he's been up, do we? Give him the benefit of the doubt. Please."

Kristy gave a slanting smile and replied, "OK. Just for you."

Chapter 23

Glen got on his phone. "Boss, Boss. It's Glen."

He had tried to get hold of DI Walters about five or six times and he'd finally answered.

"Morning Glen, what can I do for you? Must be important for you to be ringing at this time in the morning, I thought I heard the phone going, I was in the shower. What is it?" Walters listened to what Glen had to say and interrupted him every now and again.

He hummed and ahhed, finally saying, "Brilliant, Glen, now we've got something to go on. We'll have to see what forensics come up with on the trainer. Are you down there now?"

"Yes," replied Bishop.

"Give me half an hour, I'll be there as soon as I can, does Sally know?" asked Walters.

"That was my next call, hopefully, she's up. I know she was in the office late last night. She was looking up on any more information on Cyril Parks, I think she had got some CCTV from Pokes Down station. That was the ticket he bought yesterday at Bournemouth station, so she was looking to see if he got off there on their CCTV. I'll tell her to come down and meet us there, maybe she's found something out."

Glen was waiting for an answer, all he got was, "OK." And the phone went dead. Glen was talking to one of the officers, directing him to cordon off the entrance to the playground and make available parking places for forensic vans and police cars, of which there would be many.

As this was happening, he saw that Walters had arrived and was walking through the gates, showing his badge to a rookie officer who obviously had never seen him in his life and was trying to stop him going any further. He looked at his badge and let him through, Walters walked up and looked at Bishop and said, "Bloody jobsworth," under his breath.

"Now then, Inspector, he was only doing his job, you would have gone mental if he'd had let you in without checking you, and you know it."

Walters looked at Bishop with a conciliatory voice, "OK, it's too early in the morning to be thinking about that. Now, what you got?"

Bishop took him over to the trainer which was in a bush in the back of the playground, out of sight of the play area.

"Right here, Boss, tucked under this bush, about 60 cm in. I've had a look, there does seem to be something that looks like blood on the tongue of the trainer."

Walters had a look and replied, "We'll let forensics have a look and see what they come up with. It certainly looks like Amanda's trainer."

Hudson was standing behind both of them, looking over them and said, "I totally agree, it does."

They both jumped and looked round. Walters saying, "Thanks for that Sally, YOU, YOU."

Sally was laughing. "Did I make you jump?"

"You Pillock," said Glen.

"Yes."

"Right," said Walters after he'd calmed down. "Looking at this scene, there doesn't seem to be any indication of a struggle. How did he get her from Tesco's, what, a half a mile away to here, without anyone even noticing? He walked through this playground, presumably holding her in his arms, she must have been struggling, shouting?"

"I would have been if that was me," said Hudson.

Glen was looking around and said, "And don't forget it was a Sunday afternoon, there would have been loads of kids and parents here playing, surely they would have seen something like that happening."

Walters went quiet, he just stood there, he looked at where the bush was and the fact you couldn't see it from the play area, and probably because there were lots of people here, they didn't see or hear anything, they may have thought the two of them were playing. It could have seemed quite natural to them.

Walters looked at them both and said, "There are three scenarios to this. One, if she was struggling and screaming, they could have thought they were playing, it's possible. But I don't think that is what happened, I think she would have done anything he said."

"Why?" asked Hudson.

Walters looked serious and said, "Because, second scenario, he was walking her at knife point, and that's why she didn't do anything, it just looked like two people walking through the playground, arm in arm on a lovely Sunday afternoon stroll. That's why no one noticed."

"And third scenario, she knew who he was, and went willingly. Right, I want a press conference for 3pm, and I want Mr and Mrs Simpson there. Let April get them up to speed on what we've found and that I believe she is still around. Don't say alive."

"And we need anyone who was here on Sunday afternoon who might have seen Amanda on her own or with anybody else to come forward and to contact the police, or Crime-stoppers. Glen told me you found Parks at Pokes Down station, any luck with that?"

"Well yes, he did get off there and we have him going down York Place, but lose him after that. I've got Frank Ross going over today to see if he can get more CCTV from the area." Hudson said it looked promising.

Just then, from the bottom of the playground entrance, Glen could see three white-gowned people coming towards them, two men and one woman. Walters knew the woman straight away. "Hi Hillary, long time no see."

Hillary Beech was in her thirties, good-looking, slim and very bright, and so she should be, she was a forensic scientist. She had solved quite a few cases for him over the last ten years they'd been working together, and they had got to know each other well, and at one stage had been an item, but that was years ago before they had become police officers and scientists, and they had never mixed business with pleasure, not that they hadn't thought about it.

"So, what you got for me this morning, Steve?" Hillary was expecting a body.

"No body, Hillary, we've got a missing girl and we think we've found her trainer under this bush. We'd like you to have a look at the trainer and the outlying area see what you pick up," Walters said, looking at Hillary.

"Oh, is this that girl that's been in the news I've been hearing about for the last couple of days?"

"Yes, it is, anything you can find that can help us would be much appreciated, she is only sixteen, and her parents are worried sick." Walters was looking concerned.

Hilary said, "No problem. I'm on the case. I'll get this through as fast as I can and get the results to you ASAP."

Walters said, "Right, everyone knows what they're doing, I've got to go and report to the chief and tell him where we are. Not far enough, for my way of thinking, but something is going to come up very soon, I can feel it in my waters, as the saying goes. OK, off you go, happy hunting. I don't need to see you at the news briefing, myself and April can handle that, you report back tonight at 6, we'll have a joint meeting at the office."

Chapter 24

Matt was back home, the police car had dropped him off outside his door. He didn't go in, he watched the police car disappear and then opened the side gate into the back yard and started looking for the cannabis he'd thrown out earlier that morning. He quickly found it, he knew he would, no one else went round there anyway.

He needed a fix after all he'd been through that day. In his mind, he was going to get away with it, they had nothing on him, they were clutching at straws. What did they mean about Luke and his console? He told them he was always in his bedroom, and Matt was with his mates in the King's Head that afternoon.

He was sure they believed him, when he explained how he cut his hand. *I'm sure I'm going to be alright*, he said to himself again, he lit a spliff and turned the TV on and carried on thinking to himself, *yeah, it's going to be fine.*

Just then, there was a knock on the door. Who the hell was that? He wasn't expecting nobody, what time was it? Eight o'clock. He thought, *I'm not going down, don't know who it is and I don't want to know.*

There was another knock, even harder, this time he thought it was the police again, and started to go down the stairs, shouting, "What do you want, I told you all I know, this afternoon," and as he had finished saying that, he opened the door to find Maggie standing there. He looked shocked and shouted, "What the fuck are you doing here? I told you never to come here again. Quick, get in."

Maggie ran up the stairs and sat on the sofa in the front room. Matt walked in, agitated, looking at Maggie, thinking, *what have I done to deserve this?* "You stupid girl," he said. "Why are you here?" Maggie was so different from Amanda but that was what he needed right now, someone he could mould.

Maggie looked frightened. "I'd been round at Auntie Beth's today and heard that you'd been arrested and I was worried about you. You haven't been charged with anything, have you?"

Matt looked at her face and saw the fear, he couldn't help but go over to her and put his arms around her and squeeze her tight. "No," he said. "They just asked me some questions, I was there helping them to find Amanda, that's all."

Maggie looked a little relieved and said, "So, nothing was asked about us two?"

Matt looked at her again and replied, "No, why should they? Nobody knows about us, do they? And that's the way it should stay, for everyone's sake."

Matt turned to face Maggie and smiled, he moved her hair from her face and touched her nose gently, his hands moved to her neck and he started massaging her shoulders and brought her closer to him and started kissing her on her neck, softly at first, but as she became more aroused, he kissed her more passionately, they were both enjoying the moment.

Matt got hold of Maggie's head and held it close to his, asking, "How long have we got?"

Maggie looked straight into his eyes and said, "All night if you want. I've arranged to stay at a friend's, if you know what I mean."

Matt just stood up, got hold of Maggie's hand, pulled her up and walked her to the bedroom.

***

The morning post had come at Bournemouth Road, and Aaron had gone to pick it up, as he was going through, he noticed one that just said Simpson, with his address in capitals. He looked at it and thought, *that's weird*, and took it into the lounge where Beth and Luke were and said, "Have you seen this? It's just come with the rest of the post, don't know what it is, looks a bit strange."

Beth took it and read the front of the envelope, and knew straight away. She screamed, "It's a ransom letter, God, it's a ransom letter."

Aaron yanked it back. "Don't be stupid, how the hell you know that?"

Beth looked at him. Shouting even louder, "You can tell, who sends something with just your surname and writes your address in capitals? A CHILD."

Luke shouted over all of them, "Why don't you just open it?"

Beth looked at Aaron who had got the letter in his hand. He slowly turned it so that the back was facing him, and put his thumb under the seal and started pushing it along the length of the envelope. It came away quite easily, he saw the letter and pulled it out, he looked at them both, scared to open it, Beth tried to snatch it but Aaron pulled it back. "OK, OK."

He opened it, there was a pause as he read it, Beth and Luke watched as Aaron slowly teared up and then full blown crying. He threw the letter to Beth and collapsed on to the sofa. Beth looked at it and started to read it out.

I gather you are looking for Amanda; well, guess what, we've got her. She's fine at the moment but that is all up to you as to how that stays. We need £50.000 by the end of the week or you will get your daughter back piece by piece. Starting with her ears. We'll send you when and where, and oh, don't contact the police, that would be a bad idea. If you need proof, we do have her, she told us about a little bear she has on her bed from when she was ill. Isn't that lovely. See you soon.

Signed.
Your Daughter's Keepers.

"Right, that's it, I've had enough of this. Someone has got my child, I don't know what for, they want money, and we aren't to tell the police."

Aaron looked at Beth, confused and said, "Well, it's a bit late now, isn't it?"

Beth couldn't believe Aaron. "We don't tell the police about the letter, do we? Let them carry on with what they're doing, and we get the money they want, take it to them and we don't get Amanda back, it's as simple as that."

Aaron said, "Beth, where are we going to get £50,000?"

"Aaron, we'll get it, even if we have to re-mortgage this house."

Luke chipped in, "I can help, I've got about £150 in my bank you can have."

Beth got hold of Luke and just hugged him tightly, crying, and said in-between sobs, "Do you know, you're such a good brother, thanks for that."

Aaron walked into the kitchen with the letter and put it on the breakfast bar and read it again, and again, he must have read it a hundred times. It never got easier, they had his daughter, he didn't know why they had chosen her, but Beth was right, they shouldn't tell the police, but maybe they could tell April, he thought, she would understand or would she, it would be her duty to go and tell. No, let's keep quiet.

***

Frank and Phil were sitting in Poole Park just outside the tennis courts, talking about Amanda. Phil asked Frank, "How did it go this morning, any problems?"

Frank looked annoyed and just grunted, "That little bitch was nearly out of there, she's like a mole."

Phil said, "How do you mean?"

"Well, I got there this morning with some breakfast to find that half of her was out under the fucking door." Frank looked at Phil with a shocked look.

"Jesus," said Phil. "I hope you got her back inside and no one heard you."

Frank looked at Phil with a smile and said, "Oh yes, I stamped on her back, kicked her in her side and grabbed her by her hair, pulled her in, and tied her to the post, she was going nowhere this time."

Phil said under his breath, "We're not supposed to hurt her, you dick."

Frank smiled again. "She has to know who's boss, doesn't she?"

"But Frank, she's only sixteen, and that's expensive merchandise, it's got to go back in a good state, you do understand that, don't you?" Phil was trying to tell Frank to calm down, and this wasn't one of their usual kidnapping victims, their usual kidnappings were drug barons, drug people, people who owed them money or, as in this case, people who owed other people money and wanted it back. Phil, looked up. "Talk of the devil, look who's here, the man himself, the man with the ideas."

He looked at them and said, "How is she, is she alright, you haven't hurt her, have you?"

Frank said, "I had to put her in her place this morning but she knows who's boss now."

"What have you done?" He grabbed him by the lapels of his jacket and tried to lift him up from the park bench, but he had no chance, Frank was a beast, he just fell onto his lap.

"Don't be silly, you plonker, you're going to get hurt, now that would be stupid, wouldn't it?"

Phil stood up and got hold of him and pulled him up and sat next to Frank, who straightened his jacket and put one arm around Matt.

"Matt, these things happen sometimes, it's you that has this problem, you've made Amanda have a problem with this idea, and now that it's in full swing, I'm afraid you can't stop it. You owe money to a lot of people, nasty people, who want it back. Now, they're quite willing to go ahead with this because they're going to make a bit on the side, and of course, it was your idea all along."

Matt looked confused. "How do you mean, a bit on the side?"

"Well, how much do you owe Mick?" asked Phil.

"£25,000," replied Matt.

Phil laughed and said, "Oh well, that's alright then. Mick is going to make £25,000 on the deal then, not a bad profit, don't you think?"

Matt went mad. "He can't do that, how can he do that? Aaron and Beth might be able to scrape together £25,000 within their family and friends but no way could they get £50,000."

"Well, they'll have to go onto Go Fund Me, or something, they'll get it, it's their daughter," Phil said, looking daggers at Matt. "Right," said Phil, "Amanda is very safe. She is being looked after very well, what I need you to do now is to go and see whether they have received our letter?"

"What letter?" asked Matt.

"The ransom letter, it gives them till the end of the week to come up with the money or they're going to start receiving Amanda a bit at a time, firstly her ears."

Matt shouted, "For God's sake, don't hurt her."

Matt went into shock, and visibly started shaking, he could not believe this was happening, from what he thought was a simple idea that was going to get the dealer's money back, to this. What had he done? If you play with the devil, you have to do what the devil says, there was no way out.

Matt could feel tears welling up, but stopped them, he didn't want to show weakness. Why had he started this, what had he been thinking? *I need to die, now!* He thought.

Chapter 25

Cyril was standing outside 202 Gladstone Road, and pressed the intercom for Flat 4. It said Sandra Lesson. It rang once and within thirty seconds, a voice he recognised said, "Hello?"

Cyril said, "Is that Sandra?"

"Yes. Who is this?" asked Sandra inquisitively.

"It's me, Cyril, your long lost mate from Poole. Was in the area, thought I'd pop by and see how you were doing. Get the kettle on."

Sandra shouted, "Bloody hell! You'd better come up."

The latch went and he pushed the door and walked up a flight of stairs, saw number four, it was open, and walked in.

"Hello," he shouted.

"In the kitchen, just putting the kettle on," said Sandra. She turned and just looked at him and stared, looked him up and down and said, "Well, you've let yourself go a bit."

He looked hurt by that, saying, "Well, thanks for that, how long has it been? Maybe three years, and that's what I get, you've let yourself go a bit."

Sandra laughed. "Sorry, I didn't mean it, I was only joking, you're still my Bobby Dazzler and you always will be."

Cyril laughed now and said, "And so I should be, now where's that cup of tea?"

Sandra picked up a tray and carried it through to the lounge, telling Cyril to follow her. They talked about the old days, about the relationship they had had, how good it had been, sometimes, and how bad it had been, sometimes, but they agreed not to talk about those times. They laughed a lot and got serious on occasions, talking about old friends that had disappeared or died.

Then there was a pause as always in a conversation, Cyril looked straight at Sandra and said, "Sandra, I have to tell you, there's another reason I've come to see you today, and I hope you can help me."

Sandra looked at his face and knew it was serious. "Go on then, what have you got yourself into now? Who's after you, you're still not in the drugs game, are you?"

Cyril looked shocked that she could even think that. "No, I gave that up after I left Boscombe, you know after I did that favour for you and got that dealer off your back, for that money you owed him."

Sandra looked at him strangely. "Oh my God, was that you? I'm so sorry, I didn't know. He came back and told me the debt was paid and asked me if I wanted any more, I seriously thought about it, I was so close, but thought, no, I'm going to go clean and I've been clean ever since. Thank you. What can I do for you, ask anything it's yours."

Cyril paused. "Well, I need to lay low for a few days."

Sandra looked at him. "I asked you before who's after you, what have you done? Tell me, maybe I can help."

"Sandra, please, it's nothing like that. Well, it is."

Cyril went through all that had gone on over the last two to three days, that a girl had gone missing, he'd seen her come past the Tesco's where he worked but they'd come back to ask him down to the station for some more questioning, told her that he'd run from the police because he knew that they knew he had a criminal record. Sandra asked for what. He was shy of telling her, but she insisted, he relented and told her, she wasn't judgemental in any way.

Sandra said, "For God's sake Cyril that was forty years ago, they can't think you have anything to do with this disappearance, can they?"

"I don't know, and I don't want to find out," replied Cyril.

"Now listen here," said Sandra. "All I can say is the best thing for you to do is to bite the bullet and go down to the police station and hand yourself in and explain yourself, answer all the questions. You've got nothing to do with this, have you? HAVE YOU?"

"NO," said Cyril.

"Well, that's fine, I'll come down with you if you want, I'll be by your side and we can get through this together. You're worrying about nothing, I really mean that." Sandra was looking positive.

Cyril caved in, saying, "OK Sandra, I trust you with my life and we go a long way back. But can we please do it in the morning, I've hardly slept for a day, I need some sleep."

"OK," she said. "I'll get some blankets for the sofa."

Cyril looked at her with a pair of puppy dog eyes, Sandra noticed and said, "In your dreams, Cyril. I love you a lot, but it isn't going to happen. I'll see you in the morning, night."

Cyril replied, "Night."

***

April was sitting with Aaron and Beth round the breakfast bar in the kitchen. They were having small talk about the weather and how they were holding up when April started what she'd gone there to tell them, "Aaron, Beth, we need you to talk to the press, we've set up a press conference this afternoon at 3 at the police station. DI Walters thinks it can only help."

Beth looked at Aaron as if to say, what we do, we said we weren't going to say anything about the ransom note.

Aaron said, "Oh, I didn't know we'd have to do something like that, do we have to?"

April looked at them and said, "Well, to bring you up to where we are now, we think we've found one of Amanda's trainers."

Beth looked shocked. "Where? How? Are you sure it was hers?"

April tried to calm her down. "Beth, look, it's gone to forensics to be checked over, it was found in the playgrounds on Princess Road, which is close to her last sighting outside Tesco's on Poole Road. So, what we need is for you to ask for anybody who was at the playground on that Sunday afternoon, to get in touch with us."

"If they saw Amanda walking through on her own, or possibly with someone else. Beth, we need the public's help on this one, and it's going to look and sound better from you, and it's going to get Amanda back, I'm sure you want that, don't you?"

Aaron looked daggers at April. "What are you saying, that we don't want Amanda back?"

April put her hands up. "No, I wasn't saying that, but it is something we are asking you to do. If you don't want to do this, we can do this a different way, but coming from the parents always makes it a more powerful message and appeal. It's up to you."

Luke, who'd been listening in the background, piped up, "Mum, Dad, I know we have other things to think about, but we have to do as April says, it can only help get Amanda back. I want to be there too, I want to say something as well, I love Amanda, she's my best friend. I want her back."

April looked at Luke then at Beth and Aaron and said, "So, we can get that sorted for this afternoon then?"

Aaron said, "Yes, I suppose so."

But April didn't feel he was at all convinced. There was something amiss here, but she didn't know what it was.

***

Maggie was in Matt's kitchen, Matt could hear her, he thought she was making coffee, so he turned himself over and held the pillow between his legs and arms and tried to fall back to sleep. Maggie walked in with two mugs and said, "Matt, Matt," then a bit louder, "Matt, I've got us a coffee."

Matt turned to look at her, saying, "Oh that's nice, I really need that."

He pulled himself up and rested on the headboard holding his mug, Maggie went to the other side and laid next to him. They both laid there for a good five minutes, staring at anything and nothing in the bedroom until Matt broke the ice, "Thanks for last night. It was unexpected, but what a night. I didn't know you knew all those moves, who've you been practising with?"

Maggie went bright red and pulled the covers over her head, nearly spilling the coffee.

"Whoever it was, I'll have to go and thank him." He started to pull the sheet back to find Maggie with a big grin on her face. Matt looked and said, "OMG. Who was it, is it someone I know? Tell me who it was, I want to know."

Maggie just carried on smiling and giggled, saying, "I'm not going to tell you that, that's private and you don't need to know."

Matt put his mug down on the bedside table, turned and started to tickle Maggie, thank God she'd drunk the coffee. "Come on, who was it, you're going to tell me or you're going to be tickled all morning?" Matt was laughing loudly.

Maggie was screaming, "No, no, stop it, stop it." She couldn't stop laughing, she was losing her breath now.

Matt thought, *this is working*. "Come on then, who is he?"

Maggie just screamed, "OK, OK, stop, stop, I'll tell you."

Matt stopped and sat there, looking at her, waiting for her to say something. She slowly slowed her breathing down and started to tell him, "Well, do you remember when we were in the Dolphin Centre and you went off with Amanda that night?"

"Yes," replied Matt.

"Well, I thought it was me you were going to ask, not her. I was livid. I was going to beat her up later, even though she is my best friend, so I went out with Nigel." Maggie was smiling.

Matt laughed, saying, "What, that skinny weed, he couldn't blow a feather over."

Maggie had a very big grin on her face now and said, "Well, he's the guy you should be thanking."

"No. Well, you learn something every day, I wouldn't have though he would have had it in him," said Matt, smiling.

"Well, he certainly did."

Maggie laid there, as if she was remembering every second of the moment.

**

Amanda was walking up Bournemouth Road when her phone started ringing, she looked and it was Maggie, her best friend.

"Hi Maggie, you alright? How did your night go last night?"

Maggie replied, "Yeah, it was OK. Amy, is there any chance we could meet this morning, I need to talk to you about something?"

"Well, I was off to see Matt, but I can come and see you first, is everything OK?" Amanda sounding a bit concerned.

"Yes, I just need to run something by you." Maggie was hoping that would placate her. "Can we meet at Crumbles on Ashley Road, say in about half an hour?"

"Yeah, no problem, I've just left the house. I'll be there soon, see you there, love you. Bye."

Amanda closed her phone and made her way to Crumbles. It wasn't as busy as Amanda had thought. Maybe it was the lull between breakfast and lunch. It was about 11:30, so was about right. She found a table and ordered two cappuccinos, and waited for Maggie, who arrived five minutes later.

They both went through what had happened to them over the last few days, Amanda gushing over Matt, saying how wonderful he was, and that they were getting on so well. Maggie, trying not to steal her thunder, but knowing she was about to destroy any thoughts she had of Matt.

"Amy, I've got something to tell you, and you're not going to like it." Maggie was looking straight at Amanda.

Amanda looked confused, saying, "What do you mean, I'm not going to like it, like what?"

Maggie thought to herself, the only way to say this is to come right out and say it, so she did. "Amy, I really hate to say this, but me and Matt are seeing each other."

Amanda laughed, saying, "Don't be stupid, when has this been happening? He's with me all the time. I knew you were jealous, Maggie. Don't think I didn't know that it was you he should have asked out that day in the Dolphin. I could see it on your face, if looks could have killed, I'd have been dead that night. So, go on then, how long has this been going on in your fantasy world, since you were dropped that afternoon?"

Maggie looked angrily at Amanda. "You have no idea, Amy, where do you think he was that Wednesday night? I think he told you he crashed at a friend's house after drinking too much."

Amanda thought about the conversation they'd had about that, and she knew he was lying. Maggie carried on, "And that Saturday he was in the King's Head with the lads, I think that's what he told you that time, well he was, but that was later on. I was in Westbourne at his flat, enjoying his company. Do you want me to carry on?"

Amanda couldn't believe what she was hearing, the love of her life was cheating with her best friend. "How could you do this? How could you do this to your best friend?" she shouted. "You're a first class bitch, and you're no friend of mine, I don't want to know you, you don't exist."

Everyone in the cafe looked at their table in shock, and the waitress came over and asked if everything was alright. Nothing was said in reply. They both sat there, looking at each other, they both knew there was nothing more to be said.

Maggie started tearing up and with tears dropping down her cheeks, started to try to talk to Amanda, but it wasn't coming out. Amanda saw this and straight away got hold of her hands, saying, "Maggie, look, he's a bloke, this is what blokes do, let's just forget about him and get on with our lives. I don't want to fall out over a bloke."

Maggie wiped her eyes and looked at Amanda, saying, "I'm so sorry, it shouldn't have happened, I tried not to, but he's very persuasive."

Amanda just looked and said, "Now that's something I know something about."

It went quiet again, then Maggie started smiling, saying, "I'm supposed to meet him this morning at the playgrounds on Princess Road, you know the ones we played at when we were young."

"Yes," said Amanda.

"Well, wouldn't it be great, if we both turned up and confronted him; that would put him in his place."

Maggie was thinking this would be a great idea. Amanda not as much. "I don't know, he might turn nasty," said Amanda.

"What, with all those kids around and their mums, and don't forget the dads, I think we'll be safe, come on, let's do it. We need to teach him a lesson."

Maggie looked at Amanda and, standing up from the table, walked to the door looking determined, Amanda following close behind. They were walking up Poole Road. Amanda was in front and was walking at quite a pace, she was looking at her phone, when all of a sudden, this mobility scooter in front just stopped.

Amanda carried on walking and the next thing, she had walked right into the back of it, over she went and landed on the floor. This guy from Tesco's came to help and a couple of women, there was nothing she could do, so left it to them and waited further down the road until it was sorted.

Amanda rolled up, Maggie saying, "Quite a fall, should have been looking where you were going, are you alright?"

"Yes," said Amanda, "just a scratch."

They carried on along Poole Road, crossed over and went down Eagle Road onto Princess Street and saw the playground about 200 metres up the road. When they got there, they couldn't see Matt, so walked around, looking. Suddenly they saw him, he was out of sight round an area you couldn't see from the rest of the playground and the swings. Matt eventually saw them and waved, then realised it was Maggie and Amanda.

Brilliant, he thought, *well done, Maggie. I'll love you forever.*

They both walked up to him and both as one said, "You bastard," but as that was said, two guys, one was massive, the other not so, but big enough, just got hold of Amanda, one was holding her arm and the next thing Amanda remembered was falling asleep, thinking they'd just stuck a needle in her.

Well, that was easy, thought Matt as the two blokes carried her off arm in arm, looking as if she'd had a few to drink, their car parked round the corner waiting for their package.

Matt looked at Maggie and hugged her tightly, saying, "You did good, Maggie, obviously it all went well, or you wouldn't be here. I can't thank you enough, you've got me out of the biggest crap I've ever been in, they would have killed me in a heartbeat if I hadn't got the money for them, and this was the only way I could think for them to get it."

Maggie was in shock, she didn't think it was going to be that bad. She said to Matt, "I didn't want to do this, Amy is my best friend, I've only done it for you, they'd better not hurt her, or I'll never forgive you, I'll never forgive myself."

"She's only going to be gone maybe three to four days and then she will be back with us, don't worry, it's all planned out."

Matt was trying to reassure Maggie. Maggie was thinking otherwise. "What have I done?" Matt hadn't warned her about those men. And they looked awful.

Chapter 26

Matt arrived at Amanda's house. Beth looked exhausted when she opened the door.

"Hi Matt," said Beth. "Come in, do you want a coffee?"

"Yes please," said Matt.

As he walked into the lounge, he noticed that there was an air of discontent, they were all quiet, something had happened.

Matt tried to lift the mood. "How's everyone doing?" he said with a smile.

Matt had just come from the park, he almost felt bad for them, but he had to stick to the plan, he had no choice. Aaron and Luke said, "Hi."

Not really looking at him, Beth went off to make coffee.

"Do you two want a coffee?" asked Beth as she went into the kitchen.

Aaron said, "Yes please."

Luke said, "No."

"No what, Luke?" Beth was looking at Luke. "Manners."

He said, "No thanks. Please."

"That's better, won't be a minute," as Beth put the kettle on.

First thing Aaron noticed was the bandage around Matt's hand. "What you been doing there, Matt, a bit of wrist fatigue?"

Aaron was smiling, Matt looked up at Aaron, quite surprised he'd say something like that. "Ha! Ha!" laughed Matt. "No, I wish, I was making a cabinet for the bathroom and there was a glass front, I somehow dropped it, tried to catch it and this is the result."

Beth arrived with the coffee and they sat for a while, talking about what was going on with the police and Amanda's case.

Matt's stomach churned as he heard they'd found her trainer, it was in the playground at Princess Road and they were hopeful they would get something from that, be it DNA or fingerprints, as they'd found some blood somewhere on it, Aaron didn't know where.

"That can only be good news, can't it, it seems like they're getting somewhere, she'll be back very soon, I know it," Matt said, trying to hide his nerves.

Aaron looked at Matt and said, "So, what did the police want with you, I'd heard you got arrested, that can't have been true, could it?"

Matt sat up on the sofa and came right to the edge, looked at them all and said, "I don't know where you got that from, they didn't arrest me, they were asking me all sorts of questions about Amanda and me, where we met, how we got along, did we ever argue, and then, did I know where she was. Those sorts of questions."

Beth broke in, "It seems like they think you've got something to do with this, I hope for your sake you haven't."

Matt said again, "This was the start, then it was, do you know where Amanda might have gone, has she got any special places that only you and her know about, does she have a friend she hasn't told her family about? Those sorts of questions. I was helping them with their inquiries, that's all. They let me go and thanked me for all the information I'd given, and I went home." Matt was hoping that most of these lies he was telling would be believed.

"Well, when April came and told us you had been taken to the police station for questioning, the first thing we thought was, had you had anything to do with this."

Beth looked apologetically at Matt, saying, "Matt, we're so sorry, we even thought that you could have anything to do with this, we know you love our Amanda too much to let anything like this happen to her."

Matt just smiled. Matt looked at Luke who'd been quiet all through this conversation, and thought it was about time they got together, he wanted to see how he was coping, he did love the little tyke.

"Come on then, Luke, let's go upstairs, you can show me those new games you're always telling me about. If that's alright with you two." Matt looked at them both.

Aaron straight away said, "What a good idea, it'll take both your minds off what's happening out there, but don't get too loud, I know what it can get like sometimes."

They both ran for the door and pelted up the stairs, Luke getting there first, then all you could hear was Matt trying to get into the bedroom before Luke, and a big battle at the top of the stairs, that of course Matt won. Aaron looked at Beth, saying, "So much for the not getting too loud."

They both started laughing, it was nice to feel real again, even for a moment. Luke and Matt had been playing FIFA for about an hour, having a great time when Luke looked at Matt and said, "Can you keep a secret? It's a big one, but I think you might be able to help us."

Matt said, "I don't know, Luke, it depends what it is, I'll have to decide what to do when you tell me, that's all I can say, try me."

Luke started tearing up and Matt got hold of him, saying, "Luke, it can't be that bad, can it?"

Luke started talking but only got out the word, "Amanda."

"What do you mean, Amanda? Luke, I promise, if it's anything to do with Amanda, I will keep the secret. That's a promise." Matt meant what he said. "Go on, Luke, what do you need to tell me? I'm here to listen, not to judge," looking Luke in the face.

Luke hesitated for a while, then said, "Mum and Dad have had a ransom note for Amanda." Luke burst into tears.

Matt got hold of Luke and squeezed tightly. "Come here, when did this happen?"

Luke, even more emotional, said, "Yesterday. They want fifty grand or they're going to send her ears to us as down payment, or something. I don't know why this is happening, why my sister, what has she done, Matt?"

"I don't know, Luke, but I'm sure this is going to be over soon." Matt now had two feelings in his head, one for Luke, he was going through hell and he was sure Beth and Aaron were too, but two, he'd got his answer. His debt was going to be paid, and Amanda was coming home.

***

DS Hudson was at her desk when her phone rang, she picked it up, saying, "Hudson." She listened and said, "Where? In reception, I'll be straight down." She got up from her desk and ran to DI Walters' room, all excited. "Steve, Cyril Parks has handed himself in, he's at reception."

"Well, get them to bring him up, we've got a few questions to ask him." Walters got up to get prepared for the interview.

Cyril sat in the interview room, it wasn't pleasant. Painted bright white, it had three chairs in it, and one small table. On the table was what looked like a tape recorder and in the corner a camera, and it seemed quite cold. Eventually, Walters and Hudson walked in, Walters with a file in his hand and what seemed to be a CD in Hudson's hand.

They both sat down with their backs to the door, Walters opened the file and said, "Now then Cyril, before we get started, I have to caution you. You do not have to say anything, but it may harm your defence if you do not mention when questioned something which you later rely on in court. Anything you do say may be given in evidence. Do you understand what I've just told you?"

"Yes," said Cyril.

"You can also have a solicitor with you, one of your own or a duty court solicitor, it's your choice."

Cyril looked at them both, saying, "I haven't done anything, so won't need a solicitor, thank you very much."

"OK then," said Walters. "Why did you run, Cyril? It seems a silly thing to do in the circumstances. We only wanted to ask you a few more questions about Sunday afternoon?"

Cyril looked scared, he knew he hadn't been good in the past but that was a long time ago. "I just got scared, I don't know why, I may have thought that you thought I might have something to do with this." Cyril was looking at the table.

"I'd like you to have a look at the CCTV we have of the event and to go through what you said happened on that day."

Walters put the CD in and turned it on, they all watched, and at the end, Walters said, "Now then, Cyril, you said you saw it happen and you asked her if she was OK, but it seemed to you that the people around had got it in order, is that correct?"

"Yes," said Cyril.

"Let's run the tape on a bit more, see what happens."

Walters turned it on again. The tape then showed Cyril climbing over the wall and putting his arms around Amanda and cuddling her with his mouth near her ears, saying something.

"What was all that about, what were you asking her, Cyril, I'd like to know."

Cyril looked apprehensive. "I was only asking her if she was OK and if she wanted—" he paused. "There was a first aid room in the supermarket that could deal with her leg, that's all I was saying, you can see me pointing to the store, play it again."

They did, but DI Hudson wasn't convinced. "Cyril," she said, looking at the CD, "it's nice that you care so much for her well-being. So, how much did you care about the well-being of that eight-year-old you molested, tell me that?"

Cyril exploded, "Do you know that was 40 years ago, but the problem with that is, even though I'm off the sex offenders list, whenever there is a sexual offence committed in this area, you always come and question me. I'm sick of it, I try to help a girl who looked to have had a bad accident, and this is what I get. It's ridiculous."

Hudson had no pity, saying, "Once a paedophile, always a paedophile, it never goes, and that is why we check because some paedophiles who say they're cured, aren't. Does that answer your question? I hope it does. So, be ready for the next one, because no matter how far back your crime is, it will always be on your record and we will find it."

Hudson stood up and walked out of the room. Walters was a little shocked with Hudson, and looked at Cyril who was near to tears, and said, "Look, I'm really sorry that happened, it shouldn't have. My only excuse for her behaviour is her passion to find this missing girl."

"It's in all our interest, whoever is involved in the search to look at every avenue, and I'm afraid you were one. Cyril, I was watching that video, and let me tell you, I've watched it a hundred times over the last two or three days, I just saw something I might have missed, can you look at it again? You know when I asked you if you'd seen anybody following Amanda, see if you can see what I can see, is that OK with you?"

So, they watched the tape, and at first, Cyril didn't see what Walters had seen, so they watched again. Cyril said, "Stop, there, that girl, she has the same colour hair, she's slim. I don't suppose I recognised her because, and please take this the right way, I can still look at a woman and appreciate beauty, she didn't stand out all that much. I think I noticed the glasses though, reminded me of John Lennon."

Walters took another look and followed the girl behind Amanda and noticed that she was looking at what had happened and had made a move to help, and must have thought Amanda was getting the attention she needed and walked around, but was definitely looking at Amanda as if she knew her.

"Look Cyril, I'm sorry you had to go through that interrogation, but life sucks, and these are things we have to do. You set out to help this girl, and it got you into all this trouble, I hope it doesn't stop you in the future, but let me tell you something right now, I'm glad you came in, I don't think you know how much you've helped us. Can I get you a lift home?"

Cyril looked at Walters and said, "Do you know, when all this started, I thought I was doing the right thing, and in a way, I was, I'm thankful that I did, do you know why, Inspector?"

"No," said Walters.

"Because when I was on my so-called run, I looked up an old pal of mine, she was the one who persuaded me to come in, she's downstairs at this very moment, and do you know, we have rekindled something that we always knew we had, so that can't be a bad thing, can it? We're going back to her place, and we'll take it from there."

Walters smiled at him, saying, "Cyril that sounds like a good plan to me. Go and enjoy your future, mate, and let's hope we get this girl back."

Cyril looked at Walters, said nothing, but crossed his fingers as he walked out.

Chapter 27

April sat with Aaron and Beth, and Luke was in his room. He'd been told to go there, he was not too happy about that at all. DI Walters sat opposite Aaron and Beth and was talking to Aaron, "Aaron, look, we are so close, we've got so many good leads now, we just need the one that's going to bring back Amanda, and I know we will get it from this press conference."

"We need the both of you to come down and talk to the press, it can only help, I know it's a big thing for you, but there will be people there who will help you get through this, and April will be there throughout to guide you."

Beth looked at Aaron and Walters could see she was apprehensive. "What don't you like about it, Beth, are you scared of the cameras? The best way I can put this, Beth, is that they are there to help us and you, they're not there to sensationalise what you are going through and your hurt, they want to get this out as much as we do, is that OK? Can we go with it, Beth?" Walters looked at Aaron. "Aaron, is it OK with you as well?"

They both looked at each other with that look of defeat, they knew there was no way out of this, they had to meet the press, they just hoped the kidnappers knew that, and wouldn't do anything to Amanda.

Chapter 28

Matt had made arrangements to meet Maggie that night at the Churchill on Ashley Road, they'd been there about an hour when Frank, one of the kidnappers, walked in. He always looked menacing, always dressed in black, but always wore white trainers, it wasn't clear why, maybe he thought he looked the part. He did.

Matt thought he hadn't seen him, but he had, Frank had his pint in his hand and he turned to look at Matt and tipped his drink up. Matt returned the compliment and smiled. Maggie, looking at him, said to Matt, "Oh God Matt, what's he doing here?"

"You don't want to know, he's a friend of a friend, just stay quiet, Maggie, I'll do the talking."

"Well, it looks like you're going to have to, he's on his way over." Maggie sat upright.

Frank sat on a barstool across from them, saying, "Hi Matt, how's it going? Long time no see, and who's this lovely lady you have here? I don't think we've been introduced?"

Matt stuttered, "Erm, this is Maggie."

Frank looked at them both and laughed and said, "I've got a good memory for faces. I know you, love, do you take me for a great big fucking fool, I know who she is, it may have happened quickly, and it may have happened round the back where no one was looking, but don't you think we were looking at the two of you coming to us. We saw that you, Maggie, were bringing your so-called friend, Amanda, right to us, you stupid bitch."

Maggie started tearing up.

"Don't start that crap, you're in this as deep as we are, love, so long as Mad Mick gets his money, Amanda's going to be fine, isn't she, Matt?"

"What the hell does he mean, Matt, you said this was going to be easy, it would be over in a couple of days, what's he talking about? Who's Mad Mick?" Maggie was looking daggers at Matt.

"Are you going to tell her or do you want me to?" smiled Frank.

Matt went very quiet, and just looked into his pint. "Well, it looks like it's going to be me, doesn't it Matt? How old are you, girl?" asked Frank.

"Sixteen," said Maggie.

"Aw, sweet sixteen. Not so sweet, I don't think. I hadn't heard of Matt until my boss told me about him, saying I needed to pay him a visit. You see, he owes my boss a lot of money. Did you know your friend was a gambler and a druggie?"

Maggie stared at Matt, saying nothing. Frank carried on, "Obviously, by that look, you didn't, well, his gambling got him into a lot of trouble to the tune of twenty-five grand."

Maggie was gobsmacked, she looked at Matt and thumped him in the chest and got up to go, saying, "You bastard."

Frank jumped in and under his breath, said, "Sit down now! You need to hear the rest of this."

Maggie sat, but with a gap between her and Matt.

"Right, I'll carry on. When I met Matt at his flat, he was very compliant, he was going to get the money and told me that he had a brilliant way to get it. I said, go on then. He told me that Amanda's parents were loaded and would do anything to get their daughter back. I said, am I hearing what you are saying, you want us to kidnap Amanda, so that you could pay us the money you owed us, that was the crux of it, wasn't it, Matt?"

Matt said nothing. Maggie thought for a moment, saying, "So that's when you got me to get Amanda to the playground so she could be taken, you little shit, if I'd have known that, there would have been no way I'd have done that for you, I can't believe you've done this, not to Amanda, you've played us both, haven't you?"

Frank just started laughing loud, looking at Maggie and said, "Maggie, you're very young, and you've got a lot of living to do, let this be your first lesson on men, they're always out for what they can get, especially from women. Right, Matt, have you found out if they've got the letter?"

Maggie looked at Matt. "What letter?"

Matt looked at Frank and just nodded yes. Frank got up and said, "Thanks for that, Matt, that's all I needed to know, talk to you soon."

Maggie didn't know what to do, she looked at Matt angrily, she wanted to smack him all over, to beat him up, to hurt him, but just like he'd come up with an idea to get the money, she was thinking of a way she could help Amanda, but it was very dangerous and a lot of people could get hurt or even die, including her, but what were best friends for? To be there, and she hadn't been there for Amanda for a long time. Now, it was time to change that.

Chapter 29

As Phil opened the bolts and unlocked the door, he could hear Amanda scurrying around, she put her hands up to her face to block out the sunlight, and Phil realised she had got herself tangled up in the rope.

"What have you been doing now, Amanda, look at the state of you, you look like a trussed-up chicken." He put the bag of food down and walked over to her, he tried to help her get out of the bindings but she had made a good job of it. "How the hell have you got like this? Just stay still, let me see what I can do."

Amanda knew it was a different voice straight away, it was softer, more polite, nicer but he still had a balaclava on, which made her edgy. She didn't say a word and just let him get on with it, then all of a sudden, she felt a hand on her left breast, she shouted, "What are you doing?" and pulled her hands up to knock it out of the way.

He knew she was tied up, so really couldn't do a lot, so in his mind, she was fair game, and she had cost him a lot of time and money, and to him, it was payback time. He got hold of both her breasts and started to squeeze them and play with her nipples, she started to struggle, screaming, "Get off me, get off me, you fucking pervert, why are you doing this to me?"

He just laughed and said, "Because I can."

He carried on, and when he'd finished, left her in a pile on the floor, her shorts and knickers by her side, her t-shirt wrapped around her neck.

"Get dressed and stop crying, you'll be going home soon, that's if everything goes to plan, mind you, that depends on your mum and dad but I'm sure they love you enough to pay the money," he said. She got dressed the best she could, it took her forever, all he was saying was, "Come on, get on with it, I've got to be somewhere."

She finished, he picked her up and dragged her to the post and retied her. He pointed to the bag on the floor and kicked it over to her.

"There's your food for today, enjoy, see you tomorrow."

On that note, he turned and walked to the door, opened it, closed and locking it, then it all went quiet. Amanda sat there, looking into space, wondering what had just happened, she didn't want to think about it, she felt dirty. She started scratching herself to try and get the smell of him off her.

It wasn't working, then she stopped. Into her head came the nightmare she'd had, and knew that it wasn't a nightmare, it was true. She let out a scream and started sobbing uncontrollably.

Chapter 30

Aaron and Beth sat in the back of an unmarked police car on their way to the police headquarters in Poole. April sat in the front, explaining what was going to happen when they arrived. April explained that there would be press in the front and cameras and photographers at the back, not to worry about them, they were there to listen to what they had to say.

She looked at Beth who looked really nervous, and said, "Beth, you look nervous, don't be, don't forget you're here for Amanda, you're both here to get her back. Now, I've one last question. I will start the conference off with a few words of introductions, but I need to know that once you've read your statement out, do you want to answer any questions the press might want to ask you?"

Aaron said, "How do you mean, what questions?"

They arrived at the station, and walked into the family room.

April started to reply when DI Walters walked in. "Hello, you two, how you holding up?"

April broke in, saying, "Aaron was just asking what sort of questions the press might ask."

Walters walked over to the coffee machine, poured a coffee and sat down with them both, he looked at them, saying, "You never know with the press, I'll be honest with you, but with cases like this, they are usually brilliant. They'll want to get Amanda back as much as you do. Has April told you, you don't have to answer their questions, we can do that for you, if that makes it easier?"

Beth quickly said, "Yes please, it is going to be hard enough reading the statement."

"OK then that is settled then. Have you been over what the statement is going to say, April?" Walters was looking at April.

"Yes, it's all in there, and it hits all the right notes, so here's hoping someone out there is either watching or listening."

"Right," said Walters, "I'm ready if you are." He stood up and took a last swig of his coffee. "Shall we go and get this done?"

They all looked at each other, Aaron and Beth were frozen to their seats. But Aaron was looking at Beth and said, "Come on Beth, let's get this over with."

He got up, quickly followed by Beth and they both followed DI Walters and April into the press room. There was a melee of reporters and photographers there, Beth didn't expect that many, and jumped when the flash lights from the cameras went off.

"Ladies, gentlemen, please have a little respect, Beth and Aaron are not in the best of states at the moment, so can you consider their feelings, please, before we start?" Walters looked crossly at the press.

Walters pointed to a long table and directed Beth and Aaron to sit in the middle where there were at least a dozen mics in front of them. This had gone national so the big boys were there, BBC, ITV, SKY and all the local news networks. They all sat down, Beth and Aaron staring at the press as if they were aliens. Walters sat to their left and April to their right.

April started, "Good afternoon, everyone, my name is April Smith. I am the liaison officer on this case. Can I introduce DI Walters, the chief detective in charge of the investigation? Can I thank you for coming this afternoon? We are here today to ask the public to help us in finding Amanda Simpson, who disappeared last Sunday, 25th August."

"Now, we have the last sighting of Amanda, at about 1:55 on that afternoon just outside Tesco's on Poole Road, Branksome. She had had a little accident with a mobility scooter and had fallen over, if anyone witnessed that collision, or anyone who went to help Amanda, we'd love to talk to you."

"You might have seen something or may have seen somebody around following Amanda, it can only help in our enquiries. Now, Amanda left her home at about 11 that morning and the next time we see her, as I say is outside the Tesco's at about 1.55 pm."

"We have no idea where she was for these three hours, if anyone saw her, can they get in touch? They can either ring the police on 01202-222222 or Crime-stoppers on 0800-555-111."

April pointed to a photograph on the screen, explaining what she was wearing, a white tank top t-shirt with blue denim shorts, white Nike trainers and she had white trainer socks on, which had a blue frilly trim. She was also carrying a blue denim shoulder bag that strapped around her shoulders.

She pointed to a photo of Amanda on a screen behind her. "Now, I do say this again, if you think you have seen Amanda, or you have any information that can help, please don't hesitate to contact us on these numbers and help us bring back Amanda, she's been away far too long now."

There was a clamour of questions coming from the reporters but Walters raised his voice, saying, "Ladies, gentlemen, you can ask your questions later to either myself or April. I would like to introduce Aaron and Beth, the parents of Amanda, who would like to say a few words, but have asked that, after they have given their statement, that all questions be directed to the police. Thanks."

Beth looked at every one in front of her, and paused, Aaron had no idea what she had written, she had gone upstairs into their bedroom after DI Walters had persuaded them to do this press conference.

Beth looked at Aaron for moral support, he just nodded. Beth, staring at her notes, started, "I would like you to imaging what it is like to lose someone you love, you think you know they're around, but you're not too sure. You think they are safe, but you're not too sure."

"If they are with someone, that they're looking after them. But you're not too sure. Amanda is an amazing young girl, she's bright, fun loving, cares about the planet, cares about people. Things start going through your mind. Why Amanda? What has she done to deserve this? Who has she crossed?"

"No one that I can think off. Amanda has just disappeared, one minute she was there, the next gone, or that's how it seems. I hope you can imagine the total hurt in our hearts, the total gap in our lives, as well as my son, Luke, who is distraught, and wants his big sister back."

Beth was near to tears now, Aaron, seeing this, took over, "Please, we ask one thing, if you know anything, it may seem nothing to you, but it could be the one thing that brings our Amanda back to us, please come forward."

Aaron got hold of Beth, they both stood up and walked to the exit door they'd come in through, to a barrage of questions coming from the press. Walters shouting, "As I said, any questions are to come through me."

The press conference carried on, with both Walters and April answering the press questions as best they could without giving too much away of what they really had, and they both knew it, if this press conference didn't work, they were running out of leads.

Chapter 31

Aaron had been in contact with the bank, and they had told him he could get £30,000 as a re-mortgage on his house. He had asked for £50,000, but they had said there wasn't enough equity. It was a devastating blow. Aaron had about £5,000 he could get hold of quickly, but the rest were in stocks, and that took forever.

He needed to get £15,000 from somewhere, and quick. He knew now that he had no choice but to go cap in hand to anyone he knew that might be able to help him, but the problem, and he knew it would be a problem, they'd want to know why.

His first port of call was Geoff, his dad. He'd told Beth where he was going and said, "I'm sure he'll help, and if I ask him to keep quiet, he will. I mean, it's for the good of Amanda, isn't it?"

Beth agreed, "I'm sure he will, Aaron, he's got to, she's his granddaughter."

Aaron arrived at his parents' house, rang the doorbell, and his dad opened the door. Geoff, his dad, was a bit shocked. "What's happened?" he said. "Have they found her? Please say she's alive, I don't think I could handle any other sort of news."

Aaron looked at his dad and just said, "Can I come in?"

They both went in and Geoff shouted for Mary, his mum. Mary saw Aaron and said the same as Geoff, "What's happened?"

Aaron looked at them both, and asked them to sit down. Aaron started telling them about the ransom note and that they wanted fifty grand, or they were going to send her back piece by piece, starting with her ears. He was tearing up again, and his mum ran over and cuddled him, saying, "Aaron, it's going to be alright, we are going to get her back."

Geoff looked at Aaron, asking, "How much have you got so far?"

Aaron replied, "I've managed to re-mortgage the house, but they would only give me £30,000, they're saying I don't have enough equity, I can lay my hands on about five grand quickly but I'm short of £15,000, and this is why I'm here, hoping you can help us."

Geoff looked at Mary and she knew exactly what he was going to say, "Matt, that is my granddaughter you're talking about, she's the only one I've got and I want to keep it that way. I've seen her grow up to be a credit to both you and Beth. Of course, I'm going to help. Now, you can stop all that nonsense of remortgaging and keep your money in the bank. You're going to need that for your future. So, all in all you need £50,000, and when do these bastards need it for?"

Aaron couldn't believe what he was hearing, and answered, "Saturday, Saturday night."

"Well, that's easy enough, I thought you were going to say tomorrow. Now, I don't want you to think of this as a loan, I want you to think you're getting a bit of your inheritance early. It is your money, and you can do whatever you want with it, and I'm sure I know what you're going to do with this bit, am I right?" Geoff knew Aaron would do the right thing. But after all the talk, Geoff still suggested he talk to the police.

Aaron got up and hugged both of them, crying with joy, he couldn't stop thanking them. He now knew his daughter was going to be safe and coming home to them.

***

Ruth and Jack sat at home, they had just watched the latest news report on Amanda's kidnapping, and had seen the press conference that Aaron and Beth had given. They were struck by how calm Beth was, and she knew that her statement would have got through to people, because it had moved both her and Jack.

Maggie was watching it with them, and had gone to her room, visibly upset.

"Do you think I should go and see if she's alright, Jack?"

"No, leave her, I know it's hitting her hard, but I did say to her the other day when we were talking about Amanda that I was there for her if she wanted to talk."

Maggie was looking at photos on her phone, the ones with her and Amanda. She started laughing at some of them, but went quiet with the others. She went back to her thoughts of when she came out of the Churchill the other night, and the line Beth had said from the press conference.

"If she's with someone, are they looking after them? But you're not sure."

This had stuck with Maggie, she had said she was going to destroy Matt for what he'd done to Amanda, she knew she was to blame as well, but it was time to grow up, be an adult. She got off her bed, put her coat on, put her phone in her pocket, and made her way to the police station with her plan, and hoped they would accept it.

***

Matt's phone went. He'd got a text. He looked at the number, but had no idea who it was. Reading it, he thought, *what the hell?*

Matt was told to go to Smarties Sports Bar in Bournemouth and be there for 9 that night. He'd been there before, but that was a long time ago. Who wanted to see him and was that important they couldn't ring? His first thought was to ring Maggie, but she wasn't picking up.

Where was she? He knew she was angry with him, but he wanted to explain why he'd done it, and that he'd had no option, or he'd be dead; surely, she could understand that.

He stood outside Smarties and noticed that Frank and Phil were at the bar. *Shit, is that who sent the text, what do they want,* he thought. He walked in through the double doors and noticed that there must have been ten people playing snooker and about a dozen playing pool, it looked busy, he thought, for a Wednesday night, there was a piece about the US Open on the TV and there was a group of tennis fans watching and discussing who they thought might win. It was getting quite noisy. He didn't think tennis fans were so committed.

Phil finally saw him and waved him over. "Good evening, Matt, you got the message then, glad you could make it."

Matt gave a nervous smile, and said, "It didn't seem like I'd got an option. Did you send it, I didn't recognise the number?"

"No, I did," came a voice from behind him. Matt turned to see a bloke with straight black hair gelled to his scalp, he looked about 25, but he was sure he was older, from top to bottom, he wore designer clothes. Converse cap turned the wrong way, Adidas track suit, Jordan trainers, the usual gold chain round his neck, a gold ring on nearly every finger, and believe it or not, when he smiled, he had two gold front teeth.

Matt looked at this guy and thought he'd just walked out of a gangster rap video. Matt looked and thought, *what the fuck have I got myself into? They've asked me here to bump me off.* He panicked and was hyperventilating, saying, "I've done all you asked me to do, the money is coming, it's all set up for Saturday, it will be with you in three days."

Phil saw Mad Mick coming into the club and introduced Matt. Mad Mick walked up to him and slowly started tapping him on his cheek. "Calm down," said Mad Mick. "I know you've done a good job, Phil keeps telling me, don't you Phil?"

Phil replied, "Yes boss, he's been great."

"Now, I've asked you here firstly so we can meet. I always like to know who I am dealing with, and secondly, I need you to do one thing more, it won't be hard to do, but it has to be done. I have a bit of business in London and I'd like you to take a parcel for me. Now, I know you've done this before for me, but doing this will pay for all the interest you owe on the debt."

Matt looked confused. "But I thought you'd included that in the twenty-five grand?"

"Ha Ha! Well, you thought wrong, interest is charged on a daily basis, not the sum owed, it goes up every day. So, guess what, you're off to London tomorrow. If you go first thing, drop this parcel off, you'll be back for the afternoon. That OK with you, isn't it?"

Matt knew he had no choice. He had to do this.

"Phil, get the parcel, please, and meet Matt at his car. And Matt, it was nice doing business with you, nice to meet you. See you again, hopefully."

Matt got to his car and soon realised it was more than a parcel, it was a big package maybe ten kilos in weight.

"What the hell is that? That's bigger than a parcel, Phil," he said, looking into his boot.

Phil said, "Oh, you've noticed, it doesn't matter, parcel, packet, they're all the same, just one's a bit bigger. It's still going to the same place. Matt, make sure you deliver it, they will be waiting. Don't let us down, especially Mad Mick, you wouldn't want to go there, I promise."

Matt shut the boot, got in his car, and drove it as if he was a saint.

Aaron arrived home from his dad's and the first question for him from Beth was, "How did it go, did you have to tell them about the note?"

Aaron nodded. "Of course I had to tell him, he's not thick. As soon as I asked him, he knew, you don't go to your parents and ask for fifteen grand when you know your granddaughter has been missing. First thing he said was, how much do they want? I told him all about the note and what they were going to do if the money wasn't forthcoming, and he stopped me there, my dad just froze, Beth, you could see his brain ticking, then it came out."

Beth said, "What came out. What?"

Aaron knew he shouldn't be smiling but he now knew they were a step closer to finding Amanda. "He said we can have some of our inheritance, it was coming to us anyway he said, so don't re-mortgage the house, don't use our savings, we're going to need that in the future, just give him 24 hours and he'll have the money for those bastards, yes, Dad said bastard."

"You're joking me, Aaron, so how much is he getting?" asked Beth.

Aaron smiled again. "All of it Beth, the full £50,000."

Beth screamed, she didn't know what to do. She needed to ring them and thank them, but what do you say to someone who's saved your daughter? Just then, Aaron's phone pinged, telling he had a Whatsit message, it read.

"In case you thought we were pulling your leg, we've sent you this."

There was a picture attached, he opened it and staring him right in face, was Amanda.

"OH MY GOD, NO, this can't be happening, why, why would they do this? They're psychopaths."

Aaron was just looking at his daughter, he couldn't find the words. He felt numb, then the rage came, he screamed so loud, Luke came running down from his room to see his dad pulling ornaments off the shelves, kicking furniture, getting anything he could to throw at the wall.

"Dad, what is it, what's wrong?"

Beth noticed his phone had been thrown onto the sofa, and tried to pick it up. Aaron flew for it, saying, "No Beth, you can't see that, it will kill you."

Beth shouting now, "What the hell is it? Let me see, I want to see, stop treating me like a child, I'm a grown woman."

He pointed the screen at Beth, and she saw Amanda there, and she curled into a ball onto the sofa. Aaron could see her screaming, her mouth was open, but there was no noise coming out. And then, he watched in horror as she collapsed.

"Luke quick, get some water for Mum, she's fainted."

Luke ran to the kitchen, ran back and gave Aaron the glass of water. By this time, Beth was coming around. Aaron sat her up and she drank the water.

Beth looked at Aaron, saying, "What do we do, what have they done to her? She looks awful. When I find out who's done this, I'm going to kill them, and think I've done my duty."

Luke was still asking loads of questions. He was pleading with his dad to be told.

Aaron started to say, "Look Luke, at the start of this, I told you I would always tell you if anything happens. Well, something has. You know when that ransom note came, I suppose it could have come from anybody, I really didn't think of that. Well, the kidnappers have sent us something that proves they've got Amanda."

"What's that?" asked Luke.

Aaron looked at Beth and she nodded, "They've sent a picture, now I know you're going to ask to see it, but it doesn't show your sister in a good light, and I don't want you to see her like that. Now, can you trust me when I say that?"

Luke looked at his dad. "Dad, if you say it's not good to look at, I believe you, but can I ask, it doesn't show her dead, does it?"

"No darling, I promise she's still alive, and will be back with us on Saturday night." Aaron sounded convincing.

"So, does that mean you've got their money?" asked Luke.

"We need to tell the police! Look what they've done to my baby," shouted Beth.

Aaron said sternly, "NO." Aaron looked at Luke, saying, "Yes Luke, with a little help from Grandad and Grandma, I should be picking Amanda up from somewhere on Saturday night."

"That's great, Dad."

Luke got up and made his way to his bedroom as if nothing had happened. But both Aaron and Beth knew that they weren't looking after her, and they both made a conscious decision that they were going to make them pay one way or another.

Chapter 32

"Can I help you, love?" said the officer at the reception desk, Maggie was staring at the officer in a dazed state. "Are you alright, do you need any help?"

Maggie just stood there, not moving. The officer knew straight away that there was something wrong with the girl, and proceeded to go round and talk to her face to face. He put his hand on her shoulders and bent down to look in her face. Looking again, he could see she must have suffered some sort of trauma.

"Come on, love, let's go over here and have a sit down, you can tell me what's happened, OK?"

Maggie seemed to be coming round, she could hear a voice in the background, she didn't know who it was, but could hear a voice.

"Hello Missy, can you tell me your name; that would be a help?"

Maggie could hear herself saying, "Maggie."

"Well, that's a start, Maggie. Now, do you know why you've come to the police station, have you been assaulted?"

"No," she said. "I think I need to talk to someone who is dealing with that missing girl. Amanda Simpson."

The officer looked at her, and noticed she was looking a lot better, she had colour to her face now. "Right," he said, "I'll just ring through and I'm sure they'll be down soon. You just wait here, they won't be long."

He went to his desk and rang through to the Detectives' Floor, DS Hudson picked up.

"Detective Room, DS Hudson speaking."

"The officer told Hudson about the girl, and what her state was like when she came in, and that she'd asked to speak with someone who was dealing with the missing girl, Amanda Simpson."

"What, she's just walked in now?" asked Hudson.

"Yes," said the officer. "Are you coming down, she looks desperate to me."

Hudson replied, "I'm on my way, just watch her, make sure she doesn't disappear."

"Will do," the officer said, and put the phone down, he looked over to where Maggie was sitting, and shouted over, "They're on their way down, Maggie, shouldn't be more than five minutes, OK?"

Maggie looked across, saying, "Thanks for that."

DI Walters wasn't in the office, so Hudson couldn't tell him that they might have another witness. She'd tried his phone, but for some reason, it was switched off. She made her way to reception, and the officer pointed to where Maggie was. She walked over to Maggie, saying, "Hi there, I'm DS Hudson, I gather you want to talk to someone on the missing case we have, Amanda Simpson, is that right?"

Maggie stood up and looked her straight in the face and said, "I know everything, how it happened, why it happened, and who's behind it all."

Hudson just looked in surprise, and said, "Well, if that's the case, you'd better come with me and tell me what you know."

They arrived at the Detectives' Room and Hudson showed her into an interview room, asking her if she wanted a tea or a coffee. Maggie asked if she could have a Diet Coke.

"No problem," said Hudson, and went away to get it. She returned ten minutes later with DC Glen Bishop, who had been on the case since day one and knew all the ins and outs of the case. They both went into the interview room, Hudson putting the coke on the table in front of Maggie.

"Hi Maggie, it is Maggie, isn't it? Well, that's what Officer Bull said downstairs."

Maggie said, "Yes, Maggie Taylor, I'm Amanda's best friend, or should I say was her best friend."

Hudson looked at Maggie and could see the hurt in her eyes.

"Well, as you know, I'm DS Hudson and this is DC Bishop. We've both been working on this case the last few days, trying to find Amanda. So, you say you know all there is to know about Amanda's disappearance. How's that? What do you know?" asked Hudson.

Maggie told her everything, how Matt had persuaded her to get Amanda to the playground on Princess Road, how she saw two men abduct her and put her in a car. How she found out that Matt had a serious gambling addiction and he owed thousands to a top drug dealer, and had told her that this was the only way he could pay them back, or they were going to kill him.

Maggie started crying. Hudson could see it was tears for Amanda. She had known that Matt had had something to do with this all along, now she knew what. Maggie stopped crying as if someone had turned a tap off.

She looked at Hudson, saying in a determined voice, "DI Hudson, I know I had a small part in Amanda going missing, if I'd have known what that bastard had cooking, I wouldn't have gone anywhere near this, he duped me, told me he loved me, I certainly loved him, and I suppose I would have done anything for him, even this."

"Do you know something, DI Hudson, I want to help you bring Amanda home, I want to bring Matt Fisher to justice, I want to get that drug dealer as well. I want them all, I know I'm going to get my justice too, but let's get this lot in the process."

Hudson was gobsmacked, saying, "How old are you?"

Maggie said, "Sixteen, nearly seventeen."

"Well, all I can say is, you're one hell of a plucky teenager, to think this through. I'm going to have to run this by a few people, and see what they think and see if we can come up with a plan," Hudson said and started to get up from the table.

Maggie stopped her, saying, "Oh, and I need to tell you about the ransom note."

Hudson looked shocked. "There's a ransom note?"

"Yes," said Maggie. "It was delivered to Aaron and Beth two days ago, I don't know what it says, but they've definitely got it because someone called Frank came up to Matt when we were out for a drink, and asked him about it."

Hudson was sort of putting pieces together as to what they'd found out, what had been said, and also what hadn't. She had to get hold of DI Walters and quickly, they had a lot to do, lots of people to talk to, and make a plan for the apprehension of all these criminals.

***

DI Walters walked into the Detectives' Room, it was about 1pm, and wondered what the hell was going on. The place was buzzing, there were detectives all over the place. Sir Tom, the Chief Inspector was sitting with DS

Hudson, talking about God knows what, he heard one of the detectives talking to the Drugs Squad.

Walters stood in the middle of the office and said, "Right, I have the morning off, to go and see my mother, who, I have to say, I haven't seen for at least a month, and I come in to find World War III has started. Will someone tell me what's going on?"

He was looking at the room for answers. They all looked at him and pointed to Hudson.

"Sally, what's happened?" he said, looking for answers.

He was looking at Hudson when Sir Tom stood up and started walking to his office at the back of the room, closely followed by Hudson, Sir Tom saying, "You'd better follow us to your office, Steve, I think you're going to like what's happened this morning."

Walters was pleading, "What, what?"

Sir Tom sat on Walters' chair and looked at them both from behind the table. He looked at Hudson as if to say, well, get on with it. "Oh, right," said Hudson, realising what Sir Tom was looking at her for. "We had a young girl in this morning called Maggie Taylor, heard the name at all?" asked Hudson.

Walters thought for a moment, and said, "I don't think so, why should I?"

Hudson looked with a bit of a smile on her face, saying, "Well, she is Amanda's best friend, and came in this morning with a story that would have been a bestseller. It seems that she was the one who lured Amanda to the playground on Princess Road, where she was bundled into a car by two men. It also seems that the person who, as she puts it, persuaded her to do it was," and there was a pregnant pause before she revealed it, "Matt Fisher."

Walters said, "I knew there was something fishy with that lad."

Hudson smiled again and said, "Oh, there's more, our Mr Fisher has a gambling problem, to the tune of owing twenty-five grand in debt to his drug dealer, so he came up with this plan to kidnap Amanda to pay the money back to them. Oh, and the Simpson's have had a ransom note, she doesn't know what it says, but it seems as if Aaron and Beth haven't been telling us everything."

"So, what have we got in place at the moment?" asked Walters.

Hudson looked at Walters, saying, "Well, when I couldn't find you this morning, I went to see Sir Tom and discussed it with him. The first thing we did was, because it was drug related, got the drugs team in, to see if they knew of Matt Fisher, and lo and behold, he's been on their radar for a while."

"Oh, so he has been a naughty boy, what have they found out?" asked Walters.

"Well, when Amanda went missing, and they heard that it was Matt Fisher's girlfriend, they put two and two together and thought, this has got be something to do with him. Over the months, as they said, they have been watched him, followed him and he has got some new friends." Hudson was smiling again.

Walters looked at Hudson, thinking, she wants me to ask the obvious, "And who are they?" asking a bit sarcastically.

Hudson seemed to be enjoying herself. Walters knowing she was sucking up to Sir Tom, she wanted that promotion she was after, and it seemed to Walters, badly.

"Have you heard of the Boscombe Three?" said Hudson.

"I've heard of them, I haven't come across them yet, it seems we are going to do now though. Isn't their top man Mad Mick?" looking at Hudson for answers.

"Yes," she said.

"There's Mad Mick and his two main guys, Frank Bell, now we know he can be a nasty piece of work, and Phil Turnbull, we think he is second in command. They run out of Smarties Snooker Hall in Bournemouth."

Sir Tom cut in, "According to the Drugs Squad, they are the main reason there is an increase in burglaries, shoplifting, muggings and of course drug use, not only in this area but from here to London. We need to get these guys off the streets, and quickly."

Hudson looked up at Walters, saying, "Now, our plan of action, if you agree, is at 5 this afternoon, when we have all the facts, is to get together and see where we stand and take it from there, as Sir Tom has said, we need to get these bastards off the streets, and if they've got Amanda, which seems likely, get her as well."

They all got up, Sir Tom went to his office on the next floor, saying, "And keep me informed, I need to know, right?"

They both looked at him, saying, "Yes Sir, will do."

Hudson and Walters sat opposite each other, Walters saying to Hudson, "I have to say, Sally, you've done a good job putting this together. I'm proud of you, it just shows that all the talking, and training has been worthwhile."

Little did he know the secret that DS Sally Hudson was keeping from him and quickly said, "Yeah, and I have you to thank for that, it's been a blast." Sally was laughing.

"I think we can leave the drug team doing what they do. Where's this Maggie now?" asked Walters.

"Do you think we need to talk to her again?" Hudson said.

"No, she's in the cells at the moment, we've told her we're going to have to ring her parents, and she doesn't want that to happen, I told her we have no choice, you're under eighteen, it's the law. She just said, OMG, now I'm in big trouble. I just thought, you don't know the half of it, kid."

"So, the drugs team are sorting out the big boys, by the looks of it, so I think we put feelers out for Matt. I tell you what, contact him, say, I don't know, we've found something that we need his help with."

"And if he asks what, should I tell him? If he can come in, we can go through it all, and as you know, it can only help us find Amanda, right?" Hudson was looking for confirmation.

Walters was smiling. "Now that sounds good to me. Have a go, it might just work. Now, there's the subject of the ransom note that the Simpsons have got, we don't know what it says, but I can guess one thing; it says don't contact the police, that's why we haven't heard about this."

"I think I need to ask them about this, and I need to do this before the meeting at five. So, everyone knows what they're doing, I'm going to the Simpsons, you are persuading Matt to come in and that lot out there are looking for the Boscombe Three. Great, let's get on with it, it looks a lot better than it did last night. We're getting there, Sally."

Chapter 33

Luke heard a knock on the door and shouted, "I'll get it."

He opened the door to find DI Walters there, saying, "Hi Luke, are your parents in?"

Luke said, "Yes."

"Can I have a word with them, please?" looking at Luke.

Luke looked nervous, saying, "You've found her, haven't you? She's dead, isn't she?"

"Luke, no, we haven't found her, but I do need to talk to your mum and dad, is that OK?"

Just then there was a cry from the kitchen, it was Beth, "Who is it, Luke?"

Luke replied, "It's DI Walters, says he needs to talk to you."

"Well, show him in, will you, I won't be a minute."

Luke showed him into the living room. Walters asked Luke how he was holding up.

Luke said, "I miss her, I know she was a pain sometimes, but it's not the same. I want her back."

Walters said, "And that's what we're going to do."

Walters heard Beth calling Aaron, who he thought must be upstairs. Beth walked in, closely followed by Aaron.

Aaron said, "You're going to tell us she's been found, aren't you? Tell us she's safe?"

Walters looked at them all, saying, "Shall we all sit down, I've got news, some very good and some not so good. But something has come up in our investigation and I really need you to answer honestly."

"What's that?" asked Beth.

Walters again looking at them all, "There really isn't an easy way of putting this, it has come to our knowledge that you have received a ransom note. Is that true? And please don't lie."

The three of them looked at each other in disbelief.

Aaron got defensive. "Who told you that? I don't know where you got that from, they're obviously lying."

"Look, I have to tell you first that April is on her way, she is up to date in all that we know now. Once I've told you about what's going on, I'm going to have to leave, but April will answer all your questions." He took a deep breath. "Now the person who started all this is Matt."

Beth said, "What, our Matt, Amanda's Matt? You've got to be kidding, he couldn't do this, could he?"

Walters looked resigned to the fact that it was true, and carried on telling them about Maggie and what she'd done. And after every revelation that was told to them, there were replies of, "No, this can't be happening, not to our daughter."

"So, you're saying that Matt got Maggie to lure Amanda into being kidnapped, so he could pay back his drugs debt, I will fucking kill him when I see him. Does he know where she is? Give me five minutes with him, I'll soon find out for you." Aaron was looking like a lion trying to protect his pride.

Walters was trying to calm Aaron down, saying, "It would be nice, I agree, if that could happen, there have been many occasions when I've felt the same. But at the end of the day, you know and I know that that cannot happen, there are laws that say we can't."

"Now that we have this information, we are setting up a plan of action, and can I say in her defence, Maggie was the one who brought all this to us, she feels strongly that if she'd have known what was going to happen, she'd have had nothing to do with it, and that is why she has come forward, to help Amanda."

Beth shouted, "But it was her that got Amanda into this, she needs locking up with the rest of them."

Walters said, "She knew that that was going to happen, but she wanted to make amends. Now, can I see the ransom note, I know you've got it, Maggie said."

Beth said to Luke, "Go and get it will you, Luke, and give it to DI Walters."

Luke went upstairs and came down with the letter in his hand and gave it to Walters, he looked and read what it said, saying, "Well, it seems like they mean business. We're going to find her soon, before all this happens, I'll need to take this, let forensics have a look, see if they can find anything, fingerprints, DNA, that sort of thing, you never know, they might have slipped up and left something."

There was a knock on the front door, Walters said, "This could be April."

Luke said, "I'll go."

They heard a bit of a conversation going on, and then they both arrived in the room, Luke sat down, April looking, but not saying anything. Walter said, "Right, can I leave you with April, as I said, she is fully up to date with all that has happened, even the ransom note."

Aaron said to Walters, "She won't know about this."

He got his phone out, Beth just shuddering. Aaron found the pictures and gave the phone to Walters, he looked at them all, especially the one with the close up of her face, with a look that tried to say, I'm OK.

Walters was calm, saying, "I know this doesn't look good, but it does show us that Amanda is still with us, and it gives me more determination to get Amanda back. I've got to go and do what I have to do. I promise, as I have said all along, that I, or April, will tell you what is going on, no matter the outcome. Can you please send those pictures to me, there's a lot we can do with them. You've got my email address, it's on the card I gave you."

Walters stood up, said his goodbyes and got in his car, thinking to himself, these guys really mean business, they're not amateurs, these are professional, a little like a drug dealer could do. He made his way to the office for the meeting. Boy, had he a lot to tell them.

Chapter 34

Matt had arrived back from London and had gone straight to Smarties. He wanted to make sure that Mad Mick knew he had done what had been asked of him. He walked into the club to find Mad Mick sitting at the bar. He walked up to him, saying, "Mick, that parcel has been delivered."

"Well, that's good news," replied Mad Mick. "Any problems?"

"No, you gave me good directions and the owner of the garage seemed to know I was coming."

Looking at Mick for any response, but not getting any, Mick stared at Matt, he was looking quizzical. "What made you come to me in the first place? You were doing so well, earning a fortune delivering for me, then what, you thought you could do a better job than me?"

"Listen, we all have problems. Mine was gambling, you think you're going to get it back, but I've realised that that doesn't happen. I knew the money I owed you was mounting up and I had to do something, and this is what I came up with. You promised that Amanda wouldn't get hurt, but it seems from Phil and Frank that's not the case."

Mick looked at him with a wry smile. "Matt, boys will be boys. I have no say on what they do once a plan has been sorted out and, don't forget, it was your idea, and a good one at that. I'm going to get my money back and with a bit of interest."

Matt shouted, "But twenty-five grand, that's a hell of a lot of interest."

Everyone in the room looked over at Matt, they knew what was going on but didn't want to say anything, or were too frightened to.

"Have you heard back?" asked Matt.

"Amanda will be back with you and her parents by Saturday night at the latest, if all goes to plan, and I'm sure it will. I have sent a text with some lovely pictures of Amanda just to prove we mean business and where to drop the money off, so all I need you to do is to go away and hope the money arrives on time. Now, to me, that sounds like a good plan, don't you think?"

Matt said nothing, he stood up and walking to the door, saying, "If she's hurt, Mick, you'll pay, I promise."

Mick was smiling again and, pretending to shake all over, shouted back, "Yeah, can you see this, Matt, I'm shaking in my boots. I'm so scared, I'd like to see you try."

Matt stopped, turned round and looking at Mick with a red angry face, said, "I won't need to try, mate, it will just happen when you're not expecting it. Have a good and safe evening. See you soon." And he walked through the door to his car.

***

Walters got back to the office to find a hive of activity going on. He tried to find Hudson but couldn't see her anywhere. He noticed Detective Glen Bishop talking to one of the detectives from the Drug Squad, and moved towards his desk.

There were papers and photos all over the place. He recognised Amanda's and Matt's faces but there were three he didn't really recognise. He interrupted, "Hi Glen, well, I see two I know, but who are the other three?"

Glen looked up, realising it was Walters and stood, saying, "Hi Boss, can I introduce DI Barry Cauldwell, he is co-ordinating the Drug Squad. I'll let him put you up to date on what is happening on their side of the operation. How did it go with the family?"

Walters looked at them both, saying, "Tell me what's happening here, then we'll go through what I've found out, I'm sure it's going to move things forwards."

DI Cauldwell pointed to the pictures of the three photos of the Boscombe Three, pointing to the ones of Phil Turnbull and Frank Bell, saying to Walters, "These two are Mad Mick's lackies, and this one is the famous drug dealer, Mad Mick."

Walters said, "What do we know about them, how dangerous are they?"

"Oh, they're bad. Mad Mick runs drugs across the whole of the south, he has connections from Cornwall to London and as far up as Reading. We have been trying for the last three years to nab him and his associates. We've come close, but nothing has ever stuck, he's got very good lawyers and so you should when you're in the trade he's in. Turnbull and Bell do his dirty work, but again, money talks and nothing sticks to them either."

Walters was annoyed now. "We need this to stop, and now." He thought for a while and looked at Cauldwell and said, "We need to work together on this. I'm going to talk to Sir Tom, he did say I could have anything to get Amanda back and if we can get a drug cartel in the mix as well, he'll jump at the chance."

He walked to the exit, saying, "Leave it to me, I'll get this sorted, give me an hour and we'll meet back hear, say at," looking at his watch, "4.30pm, and get DS Hudson here as well, where is she?"

Bishop put his hands in the air, saying, "Don't know, Boss."

"Well, find her." Walters was getting annoyed with her again, thinking she might have her own agenda, but not knowing what it was.

***

DI Walters raised his voice to catch their attention.

"Alright. Alright, calm down. We've got a lot to get through, and not a lot of time to do it. Now, I want to bring you all up to speed on what we know so far. As you know, and for those who have only joined the task force today, we are looking for a missing girl who disappeared on Sunday afternoon at about two o'clock."

"Well, that was the last time she was seen. We now have good information, from a good source that she was abducted from Princess Playground that afternoon by the Boscombe Drug Gang."

There was an immediate shout of, "What, what the fuck, you're kidding, what do they want with her?"

"Well, it seems her boyfriend got into debt with the gang and thought this would be a great way of paying them back." Hudson had arrived to hear most of what had been said. She followed by saying that she'd been to Westbourne to see if Matt Fisher was at home, but he wasn't there and had rung him to invite him to come in to help them more with their enquiries but hadn't got through, his phone was off.

Walters looked at everyone and said, "Right, this is what is going to happen. We are going to kill two birds with one stone, we are going to set up a sting operation, one to get Amanda back to her parents and two, get the Boscombe Drug Gang."

"We need two surveillance teams, one on Matt Fisher, find him, see where he goes, he might know where Amanda is. Next, I want someone outside Smarties Club watching for Turnbull and Bell, there are a bunch of photos on the table, see where they go, they again might lead us to Amanda."

"Do this quietly don't spook them, I don't want them to know we're there, and when we want to, we can arrest them at our own convenience, got it. Report in, tell me what you see, don't do anything, I'll decide. I'm going to have a word with our main witness now, because I know she can help us, she says she wants to, let's see if she does."

Matt's phone rang, he looked and saw it was Maggie. He answered, "Hey babe, hope you've calmed down, I'm sorry about last night, you shouldn't have to witness that, it was all a mistake. Frank's a bit of a prankster, he's always getting me into trouble. I saw him this morning and gave him a right bollocking. He just laughed at me, thought it was funny."

There was a long pause as he waited for a reply, silence.

"Do you want to go for a drink tonight, maybe a meal? I'm paying. I want to make it up to you?"

Maggie didn't say a thing and was looking at DS Hudson, Walters, her dad, Jack, and mum, Ruth. They all knew why Maggie was doing this, but it was hard for them to understand why she had got herself into this predicament though they could understand why she wanted to help the police and Amanda, they knew she wasn't that sort of girl, not their Maggie.

"OK, I'll see you at the King's Head, I like it there and they do nice food, say about seven thirty, eight o'clock." Maggie was hoping he said yes.

"Great," he replied. "See you then, love you."

"Love you too," she said quietly into the phone and ended the call and laid it flat on the table, looking up at all three of them and burst into tears, saying, "I know I have to do this, but I don't know if I can."

"Don't you worry, Maggie, there will be loads of us around, I promise you'll be safe. Any problems we'll be there, on it like a flash, and we'll arrest him, OK? We just need you to get him talking about what he did and what he asked you to do, and if you can get him to talk about where Amanda is, that would be great."

"OK," she said nervously and started crying again. Ruth got up and ran round the table and hugged her tight, saying, "Darling, you are doing a brilliant job, and I know you're doing it for Amanda, and this is bound to get her back, you just see."

As Walters and Hudson walked out of the interview room, Jack heard their conversation, he didn't like it, but could agree.

Hudson said to Walters, "If she hadn't done this in the first place, we wouldn't be here, the stupid girl."

The Drug Squad's car Romeo One was outside Smarties Club, waiting for any movement from their suspects, but there had been nothing yet. They heard a message from Romeo Two.

"Romeo Two, Matt Fisher had just arrived and entered the King's Head, no sign of Maggie Taylor."

DI Walters came in.

"Anyone seen Mad Mick?"

"No boss," came the reply from Romeo One.

"Haven't seen any of the Boscombe Gang, maybe they're inside, shall I go and have a look?" asked Romeo One.

"For God's sake, no, they'll smell cop straight away. Stay out, just observe, radio in if anything happens," Walters said sternly.

There was a long pause then a call came in from Romeo Two. "Romeo Two to base, Maggie Taylor has arrived and has entered the King's Head."

Walters replied, "Right, here we go, everyone just sit tight, we'll listen to what's been said, and instructions will follow. Over and out."

The whole crew were listening as Maggie sat down next to Matt. Maggie looked apprehensive and waited for Matt to make the first move. He looked at her and thought there was something wrong.

"Are you alright, you look a bit scared?"

Maggie laughed. "What do you know about being scared, I was up most of the night going through what Frank had said, and I know you said he's a joker but it sounded true to me."

"Don't be silly, I'm sorry I asked you to help me in that way, but it was the only way I could get out of my problems." Looking into Maggie's eyes for sympathy.

"How could you do this to Amy? You led me on, you bastard, you told me you loved me, I feel used, Matt, used."

She was angry now, and wanted to hit him, but she knew she had to get the info to find Amy, so tried to control her emotions.

"I promise you that Amy will be back with us by Saturday." Matt got hold of her hands.

"How the hell do you know that?" asked Maggie.

"I just do." He got up and walked to the bar, saying, "Let's have a drink, do you want something to eat, I can order it now if you want?"

She looked up, but not looking at Matt, saying, "I'll have my usual and a burger with fries."

"Great," said Matt.

While Matt was at the bar, she could hear D I Walters in her left ear, she was connected to base by an earphone, "Maggie, you are doing brilliantly, keep him on the same path, ask him if he knows where Amanda is, this conversation is digging Matt's own grave. Try and get him to talk about Mad Mick and the boys that would help too. Keep it up, you're doing a great job."

As Matt arrived back with the drinks, he saw that Maggie was smiling.

"What's the joke?" he asked.

"Hey." Maggie realised she was doing what he was saying. "Oh, I was just thinking about last night in the Churchill, you know when that bloke came in, what was he called Fred, no Frank, that's it. He was a bit of a character, thinks he's a bit of a hard man, does he?"

"He is, you don't want to cross him." Matt was looking worriedly at Maggie.

"Why? I know he was the one who took Amy with that other bloke, what's he called, I can't remember?" Trying to get Matt to say.

"Phil, you don't want to know Phil either. He's even worse." Matt looked even more worried now.

"So, let me get this right in my head now, those two are the organ grinders, they do all the dirty work, and you don't have to tell me, but who do they do the dirty work for?"

All of a sudden, there was a crackle over the radio.

"Romeo One to base, we have movement, Phil Turnbull and Frank Bell have just left the club, we are proceeding to follow them, will keep you informed."

Maggie heard all of this in her earpiece and for one moment thought they might be coming to the King's Head, but soon put that out of her mind, how did they know where Matt was?

Matt said, "I can't tell you that."

Maggie smiled. "I think I know anyway."

"What makes you think that?" Matt asked confidently.

"Well, your friend Frank said his name in the Churchill last night, when he told me that story. You told me he was always trying to, what did you say, he was always getting you into trouble, and he was a bit of a prankster. He mentioned someone called Mad Mick, I think that was the name, am I right?"

Maggie looked at him straight in the eyes. Matt knew she was right, and gave up, blurting out, "Maggie, just don't even go there, he really is bad news. He's the one that's got Amy."

Maggie just put her hand to her mouth to stop herself from screaming, Matt quickly put his arm around her shoulders but Maggie pushed him away, nearly knocking all the drinks over. As this was happening, Matt noticed the food was arriving and said to Maggie, "Calm down, Maggie, you don't want to make a scene, do you, I'm asking you not to. Please?"

Maggie knew she had to calm down, she had one more question to ask and it was the most important one. The food was put on the table and the waiter walked back to the kitchen, turning and looking at them to see if they were alright.

Matt and Maggie sat looking at the food. Maggie at her burger and chips and Matt ate his scampi and chips, they said nothing for ages, then Maggie came out with it, "What have they done with Amy, where have they got her?"

Matt said, "Maggie, I have no idea about things like that, I'm a delivery boy, that's all I am. I know I came up with the idea and I am truly sorry I did, because it's got so out of hand. I haven't any control over what happens or what they do or say, nothing."

Maggie looked at him and calmly got up from the table, Matt watched as she did it, she slowly walked round to where he was sitting and stood right next to him and bent down next to his ear, quietly saying, "Matt, it was good while it lasted, the sex was good, sometimes. You've taught me a lot over the months. How to shit on my best friend, and others, how to have no respect for myself, how to be taken in with too much love for someone."

"But most of all to believe everything that is being told to you. I have to say, Matt, I was that girl. Now, I want you to believe what I am telling you, I want you to look around the pub and I want you to notice how many new people are at the tables, how many people you don't know. Have you clocked them yet?"

He looked around and turned his head to Maggie, saying, "Oh Maggie, what have you done?"

147

Maggie sat down next to Matt and put her hand on his knee to calm him down, squeezed it a little, saying, "Well, you know when we were in the Churchill, and I found out what you had asked me to do for you, and I didn't really know why, and I found out all the gory details. I thought, this isn't me."

"I need to help Amy, she's my best friend, you don't do this to your best friend, so I made a decision to go to the police and tell them my story and of course, yours. Do you know, Matt, they were very interested in what I had to say?"

"So, we came up with a plan, no sorry, they came up with a plan for us to meet, so I might be able to get you to talk and for you to give away all that you know about the kidnapping and where Amy might be."

Matt sat there in silence, not believing what he was hearing. Maggie carried on, "You see, Matt, I've been wired up all the time, they've been recording all of our conversation, so yes, I can honestly say I have done what I set out to do, and get a drug dealing, womanising, lowlife con off the streets."

She then looked Matt straight in the eyes, saying, "Matt, I'm not sorry for what I'm going to do or say now."

Maggie stood up and as she did, she drew her hand back and swung an enormous slap against his face, shouting, "He's ready for you now."

Matt landed on the chair, slumped over, looking up to find three to four plain clothes police officers pulling him to the ground, dragging him onto his front and handcuffing him.

"OK, OK, don't be so rough, I'm not resisting, ouch, that hurts, they're too tight, loosen them please, they're killing me."

They pulled him up and as they did, he was facing Maggie. He looked daggers at her, saying, "Wait till the gang hears about this, you never, never DOB on a drug lord like you've done, they'll just come for you, tomorrow, next week, next year, they'll just come."

Maggie looked at him with a smile, saying, "But Matt, think about our conversation tonight, I haven't said a thing, all I did, if you remember, was ask a few questions, and it seems you gave me all the answers, so you tell me, who's dobbed who in here? Think about that. Goodbye Matt, have a good life in jail."

The two officers escorted Matt to the waiting police van and took him to Police HQ. All she could hear in her earpiece were the cheers in the base room, then Walters coming through, saying, "What a job Maggie, I can't believe you're only sixteen."

Maggie cut in, "Excuse me DI Walters, I'm nearly seventeen."

"OK. Nearly seventeen then." Walters was laughing. "Do you know, I think you could teach some of my new recruits a thing or two about interview techniques? Brilliant, Maggie. Right, I'm sorry to have to do this but even after all that you've done for us tonight, you're still under arrest and as such, you'll have to come back to the station, but I promise you'll be home for breakfast."

Maggie was put in the back of a police car. And taken to Police HQ. Maggie looked out of the window; *at last,* she thought, *I have done something right.*

Chapter 35

April sat in the operations room, and was just as excited to hear that Matt had been arrested but they still weren't even close to finding Amanda, and that concerned her. She walked up to DS Hudson and asked, "Do I go and see the Simpson family and keep them up to date as to what has just happened? I think it might be a good idea, I wouldn't want them to hear it on the news tomorrow morning, you know what the press are like."

Hudson looked over at Walters and saw he was still organising the squad cars and she didn't want to disturb him, so made an executive distinction to let April go, she went off to the King's Head to mop up any last minute problems that may arise.

April arrived at the Simpson's home, it must have been a quarter after midnight, there were still lights on. She really didn't expect any less, if it was her child, she didn't think she'd be sleeping all that much. She approached the door and knocked. It opened very quickly to the face of Beth staring at her.

"I don't want to know, don't tell me, I knew she'd be dead, we had the money, why couldn't they have waited? Where is she? I want to see her."

April smiled, saying, "Beth, what are you taking about, I'm not here to say anything like that to you, I know it's late, my God, it is, isn't it, anyway, can I come in, I promise you it's all good news."

They walked into the kitchen where Aaron sat on a stool under the breakfast bar, he shot off when he realised it was April, she could see he had the same look that she had been greeted to when Beth had answered the front door, she raised her hands, saying to Aaron, "Wait a minute Aaron, before you ask, everything is alright. I've come to tell you what has happened earlier tonight."

"As you know, Maggie has been brilliant informing us about what has happened to Amanda, and tonight, she put herself in the most extreme danger to get us the information we needed to find the whereabouts of Amanda and to put

Matt into jail. She has amazed us as to how cool and determined she was going to be to get this info to help her friend and you. She's done it."

Aaron looked at Beth and wondered what April was talking about. "What do you mean, what she has been up to?" asked Aaron.

April told them everything that Maggie had done, how close she had come to Matt finding out before she had all the information, that she had been wired up, so everything that was said was got on tape. That at the end of all of it, Matt was arrested and was now in custody.

They now had a number of unmarked police cars following the other suspects, and she was sure in the not too distant future they were going to lead the police to Amanda. They would not be out of the police's sight, not for a minute.

Beth said, "It seems Maggie got her into all of this, but by God, she's helping to get her back. I've got a better understanding of her now, maybe I was a bit hard with my feelings for her a few days ago."

April said, "That's quite understandable Beth, I think we all felt the same when we first found out what she'd done to Amanda, but I can't fault her in what she's done to make amends. Look, it's getting late now, what time is it now? OMG, it's one thirty. I need to go and you need to get some sleep. I hope the news I've brought makes you feel more assured that we are doing everything to bring Amanda home."

***

April arrived back at the station. There were only a few detectives around, and she thought most must be out hunting for the Boscombe Three. Then she saw Walters at his desk, talking into what seemed to be a radio. There seemed to be a lot of noise and she couldn't make head nor tail of what it was, then she realised it was the car that was following Frank Bell and Phil Turnbull.

"Romeo One to base, we seem to be coming into Westbourne, isn't that where Matt Fisher lives? Over."

Walters replied, "Yes, see where they go and what they do, report back when you have info, over and out."

Walters saw April walking in and pulled his arm up and gestured her to come over, asking, "How did it go with the family, do they feel any better now that Matt Fisher is in custody?"

April smiled, saying, "Oh yes, I went through everything that had happened, and they were surprised at how quickly the arrest happened, last they'd heard it was still in the planning stage. I did tell them how much Maggie helped and that there was no way we could have done it without her. They've changed their opinion of Maggie and are willing to forgive and forget."

Walters thought a bit, then said, "Well that's great for the first part of the plan, we've got one of them in custody, but now need the rest. And we still don't know where Amanda is, and that's not going to be easy. Matt is a fucking idiot and is as thick as a plank. A newbie to this sort of thing. We can deal with him later; right now, I'm worried about this kid. These three are hardened criminals, they know what to do, and how to get out of any situation."

Walters looked around and saw DC Frank Ross going through some papers. He shouted over to him, saying, "Ross, got a minute?"

Ross came over, Walters carried on, "In all that has gone on tonight, did we ever check to see if there were any arms or knife offences in the past for the three remaining suspects, Mad Mick, Frank Turnbull and Phil Bell?"

Ross walked to his desk and pulled out the offences records that he had for all three of them. He looked at April and Walters, saying, "It looks to me, Boss, like all three have got some record of gun or knife crime, but they have never been convicted. They've got to have good lawyers to get out of that, wouldn't you say, Boss?"

Walters was cross, more with himself than anybody else, how could he have missed this? It's normal detective work, you should check the records of past crimes.

"Shit, I can't believe I forgot to ask the question; right, I'm going to inform the team and get an update on where we stand. We may have to bring in the Armed Response Unit, but I'll leave that for the minute. You carry on Frank, this is going to hot up in the not too distant future."

DC Ross stopped Walters from leaving, saying, "You might want to see this, Boss."

He handed him what looked like a book.

"Where's that from?" he asked Ross.

Ross replied, "Well, when I was looking for DS Hudson, I thought she might have left a note or something to let us know where she was on her desk. While I was looking, I found what I believe to be Amanda Simpson's diary, it seemed to be hidden under a lot of other books, felt a bit strange to me, don't know what you think?"

Walters opened the diary and started reading, it was nothing special, it had the usual teenager's rubbish. He finally turned to the 5th of August and read.

Met with Matt this morning, was a bit off with me, don't know what I've done, says he loves me, but he's not showing me. I think he's got someone else.

WEDNESDAY 8TH AUGUST

Supposed to meet with Matt tonight, but he's cancelled.
Said he stayed at a friend, had too much to drink.
Slept on the couch. Don't know if I believe him.

SATURDAY 11TH AUGUST

Had a great day with Matt, went into Poole, met up with Maggie, had a brilliant time, got drunk at the Kings Head, went back to his and made love all night. I love him so much.

WEDNESDAY 16TH AUGUST

What the hell is happening? Maggie is a bitch, telling me that Matt doesn't love me. Well, that's what he's told her. They seem to be talking a lot together.

SATURDAY 20TH AUGUST

Confronted Matt about what Maggie had said. He denied it all, told me to stop being stupid and he was looking forward to going out for a meal tonight. I do believe him. I do.

SUNDAY 21ST AUGUST

Asked Matt about his drugs and gambling, I knew it was affecting him, and it was affecting our relationship and it needs to stop. He was not too pleased.

Walters turned the page, there was nothing more after the 21st August, why didn't Hudson bring this information to him, why was she hiding this? Maybe it was going to implicate her in the future. He thought they had a good connection, they had worked well together, understood each other, but he would never, never sanction a cop that was bent, ever.

He walked to the radio console, pressing the to all switch, saying, "Base to all surveillance cars, report in your positions, over."

First to come in was Romeo One, "Romeo One to base, we are arriving outside Matt Fisher's flat, and we can see one of the suspects trying to contact someone on his phone, I would presume it's Fisher, he is looking up at the flat, it's in darkness, so I would hope they would know he was out. Over."

Romeo Two came through, saying they were in the station, booking in Matt Fisher.

Walters asked if DS Hudson was with them.

The reply was again confusing to Walters, "Romeo Two to base. DI Hudson was at the scene, but soon after it was all done and dusted, came up and said, she was off now, she had somewhere to be and got in her car and left. Over."

"Did she say where she was going? Over," asked Walters.

"Not a thing, Boss, she just went. Over."

Then Romeo Three came in. They were backup for Romeo Two, when they left Smarties to follow Turnbull and Bell.

"Romeo Three, just to let you know that Mad Mick has left the club, we will follow and report in as needed. Over and out."

Walters sat at his table, going through what had happened in the last few hours, he got a pen and started writing:

1. Fisher arrested at King's Head. In custody.
2. Turnbull and Bell left the club, went to Fisher's flat.
3. Mad Mick is on the move, don't know where.
4. DI Hudson has just disappeared, again.
5. The Simpson family are fully aware of what is going on.

"I think I've got it all down now. I need to wait and let it all play out," he said this under his breath, in deep concentration. "It's coming together, I think."

Chapter 36

DS Hudson arrived at the lock-up and slowly opened the door to where Amanda was being held. She held her torch up and turned it on to find Amanda fast asleep on the floor, in a crumpled mess with ropes all around her. She couldn't believe how she looked and was shocked.

Frank and Phil had gone too far this time. She had told them no violence. She walked over to where Amanda was sleeping, saying, "Amanda?" There was no movement, nothing; for one moment, she thought Amanda was dead. "Amanda?" shaking her this time. "Amanda, wake up, it's time to go. You're safe now."

Amanda slowly opened her eyes, she was in a daze, didn't know what the hell was happening, she tried to sit up but the rope stopped her. Hudson helped get the ropes off her, saying quietly to Amanda, "Amanda, my name is DS Sally Hudson, I'm with the police. I'm here to get you out of here and get you home. I know your mum and dad can't wait to see you."

Amanda was very confused, she looked outside and could see it was still dark. "Where am I? How long have I been here? Who are you? You're a woman, it's been men before." She was now getting her bearings.

Hudson moved the torch up and down Amanda's body, saying, "What have they done to you? Are you hurt anywhere?"

Amanda looked at her again, saying, "Who are you, and why are you here?"

"Amanda, look, the police found out where you were being held, it came over my radio. I was near, so I've got here first, the others will be here soon, I'm sure, but you look absolutely awful. I need to get you to a hospital and fast, just wait there, I've got a coat in the car, I'll go and get it for you."

Hudson left to go and get the coat, leaving the door open. Amanda saw this and couldn't believe her eyes, she crouched up onto her knees and pulled herself up with the pole, steadily trying to walk to the door. She could see trees and fencing and a little gravel road, lit up with the car's lights, she felt very cold and light headed and very unstable on her feet.

Where am I? She thought. Getting to the door, she realised she was in a wood, but nearby was a fence, one of those metal fences they have round buildings and security for keeping people out. Over the fence was a train with carriages, then she saw another.

As she got further out, there were loads of trains, lit up as if they were in storage. She realised then what all that noise had been early in the morning and last thing at night; trains, she had been near a train station or a stockyard.

Hudson came round the corner of the hut, saw Amanda there and said, "What are you doing, girl, you're far too weak to be walking around like that. Here, put this coat on and we'll go to the hospital in my car. It's the best thing for you. OK, just hold on to my arms, we'll get you in the car and we'll be there in no time."

Amanda did as she was told, asking, "Are my mum and dad going to be there?"

Hudson said, "Yes of course, we've got a car picking them up right now, I've been told, they can't believe you've been found, they are so happy they can't get to the hospital any faster than they are."

Amanda got into the car, Hudson started the engine and off they went. Amanda was fast asleep within minutes, laid out on the back seat, not a clue of what was going on, but safe at last.

***

Phil and Frank knew that Matt wasn't in, and tried him on his phone again. No answer.

"I think I'd better ring Mick, tell him that we can't find Matt," said Phil. "See what he suggests we do."

"Sounds like a good idea," said Frank.

"Tell you what, why don't we go down and visit the girl, have a bit of fun before she leaves us?" Frank looked at Phil with a pleased, disgusting smile.

Phil said, "Let see what Mick says and we'll take it from there, but I like your idea."

156

Phil came off the phone, saying, "Mick had told me to just leave it, we'll sort it out in the morning. We might as well go home and he'd see us at the club tomorrow lunchtime."

Frank was driving, they arrived at the woods and slowly drove down the track to the hut. All of a sudden, Phil noticed the hut door looked open, just a little, but it looked open to him.

"Frank, can you see what I can see? Oh fuck, I hope she hasn't escaped, we are dead if she has."

They got to the hut and found no Amanda. Frank said, "Where the fuck has she gone, she could be miles away by now, we've got to find her, and quick."

***

"Romeo Two to base, Romeo Two, are you reading me? Over."

"Loud and clear, go ahead, Romeo Two. Over," replied Walters.

Romeo Two came back, "We have been following the suspects, they have gone from Matt Fisher's flat to a wooded area just off the ring road. It looks a prime place for a hideout, maybe to hide someone as well. They've gone down this track into the woods. Should we follow? Over."

Walters was thinking. "Romeo Three, where is your position? Over."

"Well, it looks like we're going to Upton Country Park, we're on the A350 that's the only place I can think of that's this way. He might be going to Blandford, don't know, do we follow him, Boss?" asked Romeo Three.

Walters came in straight away, "Follow at a distance, don't give the game away, but keep me informed if anything happens. Over and out."

Walters was back onto Romeo Two, "Romeo Two, this is base, are they still down the track, and if they were to come back up, could you pen them in? Over."

"No problem, Boss, if we wait at the top, there's no way out for them. Over."

"Great," said Walters. "I'm getting you more support, and dog patrol, you might need them if they start to run. Over and out."

Things were happening, Walters would have loved to be out there, but he knew he had a good team. But where was Sally, her phone was off, Walters couldn't get her on her radio, maybe it had run out of juice. She had a lot of explaining to do when he saw her, that was for sure.

He organised the back up for Romeo Two and then asked Ross to make a coffee, he was parched, and with all that was going on at the moment, he needed a caffeine rush.

***

Phil and Frank had gone through the hut and couldn't see hide nor hair of Amanda. They had to find her, so decided to split up and search the woods. "Ring me if you catch her and I'll do the same, she can't have gone far, she was too weak to go anywhere," Phil said.

So, Frank went left and Phil went right, they both thought it was a good idea at the start but they soon regretted it. The backup arrived at the top of track and it was decided to keep one car blocking the exit and the rest would, with the dogs, help comb the area on foot. All of a sudden, one of the dogs heard some noise ahead and was chomping at the bit to investigate.

"What is it, boy, what do you hear?" The dog handler let it go, saying, "Go on, find."

The dog scampered off into the bush to find his prey and within two minutes, there was a hell of a commotion with the dog barking and a bloke shouting in pain, "Get this bloody dog of me, he's tearing me apart."

The dog handler arrived, shouting, "Leave. Leave now." The dog stopped and the handler was shouting, "Get on the floor, get on the floor, now."

As this was happening, two officers who were further down the track, saw another man who was trying to pelt it down the track. They saw him get into his car and drive up the hill at speed, an officer radioed through to say he was on his way and to be prepared.

The team at the top knew there was nowhere to go, but it seemed the driver had different idea. He floored the engine and sped towards them. He must have been doing sixty miles an hour when he crashed into the police car.

The problem was, in his haste, he had clearly not strapped in, so the next thing the officers saw was a body flying through the windscreen, into the air and landing on the other side of the car in a not so nice heap. Soon after he landed, the car started to break into flames and everyone scrambled to get away. Both cars were now write-offs.

The police didn't have to cuff him, he was too badly injured for them to even think of that. The other suspect was brought out from the woods, handcuffed, with blood running down his left leg where the dog had bit him to stop him running off. He was not a happy chappy, and all he could say was, "I'm going to sue you bastards for this. Look what that dog's done to my leg."

Sargent Pitt looked, saying, "Never mind, it will get better, I'm sure. See you in court, mate."

The rest of them watched as he was put in a police car, and the other lay there in pain, waiting for the ambulance. One of the officers came out of his car with the photos of the suspects, he walked up to the guy that was lying on the ground, not really saying much, looked at his face then the photo.

He said, "Well hello, Mr Frank Bell, nice to meet you. That was a stupid thing to do, wasn't it? We'll have to get you some driving lessons for when you get out of jail. Mind you, that's going to be a long time."

Sargent Pitt was looking at his colleague standing next to him. He made his way to the police car, hearing the other man that had been caught shouting and screaming. He again looked at the photo, then the man in the car, and thought, *That's Phil Turnbull, we've got them.*

He looked around, saying, "OK you lot, great work, now let's get these scumbags to hospital, and don't let them out of your sight. Have they been read their rights?"

"Yes, Sarge," said an officer who was holding Turnbull, trying to keep him still so there was no more damage to his leg.

The two officers who had watched the car travelling at speed up the track had made it to the bottom and noticed the hut. They called the sarge down to have a look. They all walked in, they couldn't believe what they saw. The first thing was the smell, someone had been in there a while, there was a bucket to piss in and all the rest that goes with that.

Food cartons were all over and rope strewn all over the floor. It was not a good place to be. The Sargent shook his head. He had a daughter the same age as Amanda. The thought of her being here, it made him feel sick to his stomach. Where was Amanda now? He hoped somewhere better. They left it for forensics to deal with, turned round and closed the door.

Walters was at base going mad, calling through and not getting any answers, "Come in, Romeo Two, what the hell is happening? Have you got them arrested? Come back, Romeo Two, come back anybody. Over."

All of a sudden, his radio crackled and he heard, "Romeo Two to base, Romeo Two to base, suspects arrested, one has a leg wound from one of the dogs, the other was badly injured after a car crash, they're both going to hospital when they arrive. Over."

Walter was frantic now. "Was the girl there? Over," he asked.

"Romeo Two to base, that's a no, sorry, she has been here, I can safely say that. We need forensics up here quickly. I'm sorry it's bad news, Sir, but I definitely think she's alive. It's just where. God, we were so close, Boss, so close. Over and out."

***

Hudson was in her car, making good progress down the A350, taking care to stay just under the speed limit. She didn't want to attract any attention. Amanda fast asleep in the back. Suddenly, her burner phone rang. She picked it up from the passenger seat and knew it could only be one person ringing her, she opened it and put it on loudspeaker, saying, "Hi Mick, I've got Amanda for you, where do you want her?"

Mad Mick was elated, and told Hudson he was outside the Welcome Centre in Upton Park and would wait until she arrived. It was nearly dawn when they met in the carpark. Mad Mick got out of his car and walked to Hudson, who was by her car, sitting on the bonnet. Mick was looking at her, asking, "Where is she?"

Hudson nodded towards the car. "She's fast asleep in the back, she has no idea what's happening, she thinks she's off to the hospital to get sorted and see her mum and dad."

"That's great news," said Mick. "Heard anything from Phil and Frank?"

Mick looking at Hudson, seeing a strained look on her face, and knew from that look, there was something wrong. "I know that look, what's wrong?"

Hudson knew he was going to hit the roof, but there was no way she could make this any easier. She looked at him as if to say, you're not going to like this. Hudson started, "Well, I've been listening to this all night. First, they have arrested Matt, and secondly, they've got Phil and Frank too."

"I've been trying to get hold of you for ages, my radio's been going off, my mobile hasn't stopped. Steve has been calling me every ten minutes, trying to find out where I am, I know he has, but I've not answered any of it, I've kept quiet. What the fuck are we going to do, Mick, I've been helping you all these years, and when I need to talk to you, you didn't answer, where were you?"

Mick could have kicked himself, he'd had a meeting with some of the other drug lords, someone had been trying to sell drugs cheaper in his patch and not only in Poole and Bournemouth, but Cornwall as well. He wanted it stopped, and right now.

He told Hudson what had been happening, she said, "What the fuck Mick, I think this is going to cost you more than a few dealers trying to undercut your prices. They're onto you, Mick, and they have a very good witness who knows everything."

"Who could that be? I can always get him to shut up, can't I?" sounding cocky.

Hudson looked at him with contempt, saying, "It's not going to be that easy this time, Mick. I know you've done this in the past, sent the boys to have a word, or offered money, but this girl has got a purpose in life and that's to get Amanda Simpson back. You really do have a problem. One of Amanda's mates, a kid, Maggie, has told them everything. You will need to fix this."

Mick could feel he was getting mad, he came up to Hudson and got her by the neck, choking her. "You little shit, I've a good mind to kill you." Still holding her throat, he started to tell her what was going to happen, "You are going to help me make a video to send to her parents, and this time, they won't go to the police because I will make it clear they have three hours to get the money, or they will never see her again. Get her out of the car, now."

He let go of her throat, and Hudson fell to the ground, holding her neck and gasping for breath. Trying to say something but not getting it all out. Mick heard, "You'll not get away with this, they'll get you in the end."

He picked her up, shoved her to the car, saying, "Get on with it, we haven't got all day."

Hudson looked at him. She'd had enough of him calling the shots. But he knew too much about her now, and if the police knew her working with him, she'd go to jail herself. And no one there was kind to coppers. She had no choice.

Hudson went to her car, opened the back door. Amanda was stirring. Was she awake? Had she heard any of their conversation? Amanda was stuck to the seat, not moving, looking around, afraid to say anything.

Mick shouted, "What's taking so long?" He pushed Hudson out of the way and got hold of Amanda's legs, trying to drag her out of the car but Amanda was having none of it, she managed to get one leg free and kicked Matt in the face.

There was a loud scream as Mick held his nose as streams of blood came down his face.

"You little bitch. Right, this has gone on too long," he said, and got his knife out and pointed it at Amanda's stomach, saying, "Right, we can do these one of two ways. You can get out of the car or I will use the knife to persuade you. Your choice, girl."

Hudson had got up from the floor and looked at Mick, then at Amanda. She knew she had to get her out of the car, knowing what Mick was saying, would be exactly what he would do. She got hold of Mick, saying, "Mick calm down, she's coming, can't you see she's trying? Get out of her way and put the knife away, that's not going to achieve anything."

Hudson looked at Amanda as Mick pulled away. "OK Amanda, you need to get out of the car. Please don't make him cross again, it's not worth it."

Amanda started getting out of the car, she'd more or less done it, when Mick got hold of her by the t-shirt and stood her up. He went round the back of her and held her tightly round the waist. Mick told Hudson to go and get his balaclava and bring it back to him. This she did.

"What are you going to do now?" she asked.

He went into his pocket, got his mobile out and threw it at Hudson. "Get ready to take a video, tell me when you're ready."

He put his balaclava on and waited, Hudson opened the phone and found where to take a video from and pointed it at Mick. "Ready," she said.

Mick got hold of Amanda by her hair and pulled her close to him. Looking at Hudson, he could see she wasn't liking this. Mick shouted, "Don't you dare turn that off or drop it, we're both in this together, right?"

He started talking into the camera, "Hello Simpsons family, it's me again. As you can see, Amanda is still with us, but not for long."

He got the knife out of his pocket and quickly put it to Amanda's throat. Amanda screamed, but couldn't move. She couldn't believe what was happening to her.

"Now then, I've decided not to send you her ears if you don't pay me the money, I know you will have got it by now. This is where I want it putting, on the front in Poole near the RLNI is a white boat on display, I'm sure you know it. Well, take the money there and leave it under the boat."

"I hope you've got that, and if for one moment, you're thinking of telling the powers that be, it won't be her ears I send, it will be something that will remind you of your daughter; her fucking head. Oh, and you have until noon to get this thing done."

"I promise you when I have the money, you will get your Amanda back. Turn it off now, will you? I think they will get the message."

Just before it went dead, they could hear Amanda crying, saying, "Help me Daddy, I don't want to die, please help."

He took the knife away from her throat, shouting, "Shut that noise up, I hate crying."

Amanda fell to the floor, trying to stop crying, Hudson ran up and tried to get hold of her, but Amanda pulled away, shouting and saying, "You get off me, you bitch, you're no police detective. Well, not the ones I have ever known, you're as sick as he is. No, worse, you brought me here, you knew exactly what was going to happen, how can you live with yourself?"

Mick looked across at them both, saying. "My God, she's got a lot of attitudes for a, how old is she, sixteen-year-old. Well done girl, I like a bit of spunk in my girls and please take that the right way."

Amanda looked at him in disgust, turned round and spat in his face. Mick used his shirt sleeve to wipe it away, walking off in an angry mood, thinking, *I'll leave her alone, she's worth fifty grand to me, and that will be a good day at the office, thank you very much.*

***

"Romeo Three to base, Romeo Three to base, are you receiving? Over."

Walters was giving the situation so far to Sir Tom, who was highly delighted with the outcome, praising Walters and all the teams that were involved.

"Excuse me, Sir Tom, I have to get to ops, there's a call coming through."

Walters was leaving and arriving at the radio mic to hear, "Romeo Three to base, are you receiving? Over."

Walters came in, "Reading you loud and clear, where are you? Has Mad Mick gone to where you predicted? Over."

Romeo Three couldn't contain his excitement but also shook at what he had just seen.

"Sir, you are not going to believe what we have witnessed. We followed Mad Mick into Upton Park, he is about two hundred yards in front of us, he's stopped near the tree line of the Welcome Centre near the carpark. He's sat there smoking in his car, he's been there ten, fifteen minutes when another car has arrived and parked close by."

"Mad Mick got out of his car and walked towards the other car, and just as he was on his way, a woman got out and sat on the bonnet of her car. They talked for a good ten minutes, Boss. The shit hit the fan. Mad Mick got hold of this woman by the throat, I thought he was going to kill her. We were about to fly down there and stop him, when he stopped."

Walters cut in, "Romeo three, do we know who the woman is? Over?"

Romeo Three came back with a very clinical reply, "Boss, I can't make her out at the moment."

Walters went quiet, saying nothing.

"Are you there, Boss? Did you miss what I just said?" asked Romeo Three.

"Can you get any closer, have you got your binoculars, try them?"

"Yes," said Romeo Three, "I'll check. Boss, you're not going to believe this, it's DS Hudson. Have you sent her there to negotiate Amanda's release?"

"Don't be a silly sod, Romeo Three, how did we know he was going to Upton Park? All I can think of is that Hudson has something to do with the kidnapping. Right, I have backup on the way coming to assist, more feet on the ground, ambulance, Firearms Squad and dogs, and I'm coming up to take overall command. We will arrive with no blues and twos, don't want to frighten them, do we? Over."

Romeo Three came back, "There's more, Boss. It started to get a little lighter and the next thing we saw was Amanda Simpson being dragged out of the car, held by Mad Mick with a knife against her throat and Hudson videoing the whole thing. Over."

"Right, that seems to me like they're sending the final ransom note on where to send the money, and they're making sure the Simpsons get the message. Wait till I get there and we'll have a look and see what plan we can come up with," replied Walters.

Chapter 37

Walters went into his office to find Sir Tom still there waiting for another update, he sat opposite and went through every detail. "Now, there are one or two things we can do. One, take them where they are now, or go and talk to Aaron Simpson, find out what the video says. I'm sure it tells them where to drop the money off, and nab them there. What do you think, Tom?"

Tom looked at Walters. "Now that's a tricky one, have we got everyone in place at Upton Park?"

"They'll be set up in about ten minutes, Boss."

Walters knew what the answer was going to be. "Right, you get up there, Steve and sort this out. I want this girl back with us this morning and those two in custody especially that bent copper, Hudson. She is the lowest of the low. We haven't got time to go and find where the money drop is and get that secured, all our eggs are up at the park, there's no time to change it, go and get those shits now."

Sir Tom looked angry, Walters had only seen Sir Tom like this a couple of times, and he was getting frustrated with the progress.

***

Walters arrived at Upton Park to find an array of vehicles parked on the road well away from the Welcome Centre. They were hiding in bushes, behind dustbins, the Firearms Squad had made their way round the back of the centre and were laid in wait, ready to shoot if they had to.

The time had got to 5 in the morning and Walters could see all that was going on in front of him, he could see the two cars. Mad Mick and Hudson were talking in front of the cars but he couldn't see Amanda, he thought she was in one of the cars. He radioed to all the teams to be vigilant and told the Firearms Squad not to fire unless they had a clear shot and only on his say so.

Walters realised that there were a couple of dog walkers in and around the area, and he needed to get them out of the way, so got some of the detectives to slowly walk up to them and move them on, thinking to himself, *who the hell walks their dog at 5 o'clock in the morning?*

Both Mad Mick and Hudson didn't realise what was going on, thank God, they were too deep in conversation. Walters walked back to the Control Base and met with his other detectives, DC Glen Bishop, DC Frank Ross, and DC Robert Moore, telling them the plan of action.

"Right everybody listen, this is what is going to happen, I'm not bothered about Mad Mick or DS Hudson, they've made their bed, it's time they laid in it, we are here to get Amanda Simpson back to her mum and dad and that is what we will do. Right?"

Walters looked at them all. "Now, we know Mad Mick has a knife, but we don't know if he has a gun, knowing him, he will have, so proceed with caution, I want us to drive up in three unmarked cars as if we are visiting the park, and I want one to go to the left of them, one to the right and I will stop right in front of them, stopping them from getting anywhere with their vehicles. Hopefully, the surprise will catch them off guard, we can contain them and arrest them. Have you all got it?" he asked.

"Yes boss," they replied.

Over the radio came a message, "Romeo Three to base. Over."

Walters replied, "Base to Romeo Three, reading you loud and clear."

"Romeo to base, we have a problem, the suspects are making their way to their vehicles, looks like they're leaving. Over."

"Shit," said Walters. "Let's go now, and quick, we've got to stop them, we've come too far for this to go wrong now."

They rushed to their cars, they were only about two hundred metres away, but it felt like two hundred miles. As they approached, they could see Hudson getting Amanda out of her car and transferring her to Mad Mick's car. They both heard the commotion.

Hudson was the first to react, jumping into her car and trying to flee, Walters was too quick and rammed into her driver's side door, the car swung round and stopped dead, Hudson was a bit dazed but slid across the front seats and got out the passenger door.

She legged it across the carpark, heading for the bushes to see a field of her fellow colleagues coming out. She stopped and turned around to find Walters standing right behind her. He looked at her, saying, "Good morning, Sally, you've been busy. I knew there was something happening with you, but I couldn't put my finger on it. I certainly didn't think it was this. You've always known I hate bent cops, you've been doing this for how long?" He looked at her and said softly, "Why?"

He got his handcuffs out, read her, her rights and put her in his car for safe keeping. Mad Mick, on the other hand, had decided to get a hold of Amanda and had now produced his knife and had it round her throat again. He had backed up to his car and was trying to get her into the car, but he found it hard to do this, with holding the car door open and holding Amanda at the same time.

He had to let her loose for a split second. Amanda took advantage of this and pulled all the strength she had left in her body and pushed Mad Mick into the car. He landed on the back seat and she ran for her life. Walters ran forwards as did Bishop.

Walters went to the back door where Mad Mick's head was, opened the door and got hold of the arm with the knife in it, he started ramming the arm against the middle door frame, all he could hear was Mad Mick screaming as Bishop started squeezing his bollocks, saying, "Drop the knife. Drop the knife, you bastard."

Walters eventually got him to drop it after getting him by the throat and nearly killing him. They got him out of the car, handcuffed him, read him his rights and he was put into a van that came up from the Control Base.

Walters was frantically looking around for Amanda, but couldn't see her. Then he spotted her, she had a blanket round her shoulders and an aluminium foil cape over that. She sat in the back of an ambulance, looking absolutely numb, shaking, as if she was not in this world.

Walter's thoughts were that Amanda was going to need a lot of time and counselling to get over this, but first, they had to get her to hospital, and then they would need to tell her parents the good news. Beth had always asked from the start, "Where is Amanda?" He could now tell her she was coming home.

***

"Right Hudson, you can get out now, it's time for your fifteen minutes of fame."

He got hold of her arm and helped her get out, not trying to hide the fact that it was DS Hudson who was with him. Hudson was trying to get inside as fast as she could, saying to Walters, "You're loving this, aren't you? Is it giving you a good feeling, doing this in front of the press?"

Walters looked at her, saying, "Do you know Hudson, in a way, yes, because they can see your face and will be wondering what the hell is going on. But in another way, I have to say no, because the one thing that I have hated all my police career are bent cops and you are going to cause so many problems for normal law abiding police officers who live by the code."

"We're here to serve, we are asked by the public to keep them safe, and you have just shit on a lot of the public, and of course, Amanda and her whole family. I can't imagine why?"

She replied sarcastically, "Oh, you will never understand, things take their course and suddenly you can't stop them, even if you want to. And my God, I have tried."

Walters gave the most disgusted look and squeezed her arm a little bit tighter, saying, "Well, you didn't try hard enough, did you? And now, you're going away for a long time and I can't wait to put you there."

They carried on walking through the doors, up to the charge desk where Walters read out all the charges to the booking Sargent, who was looked absolutely gobsmacked, he kept looking at Hudson in disbelief, but was professional and did his job, booked her in and directed them to take her to cell three.

Walters asked the Sargent, "Have the other two arrived?"

The Sargent said, "They're in cells one and five."

"Thanks for that, you have one more on his way, Mad Mick shouldn't be long, he got a little aggressive and we had to restrain him. He's at the hospital being seen to, I'm sure he'll be OK in a few days." Walters was laughing.

He had told everyone involved in the case to meet in the Detectives' Room at 3:30, they would have to come up with a plan of action, who was going to question who, and try to get as much information as possible. They only had 24 hours to keep them there, so they had to be on the right page from the start.

***

Aaron was out the front of his house on Bournemouth Road tending to his garden when he noticed two cars roll up, April in one of them, and DC Glen Bishop in the other. He stopped what he was doing, watching them both getting out of their cars, the difference was they were both smiling.

Aaron put his garden fork down and rushed into the house, shouting, "Beth, Luke, the detectives are here, there are two cars outside."

By the time all the family were in the lounge, April and DC Bishop had walked in to see the look of fear on all their faces, she couldn't hold back saying in a very happy voice, "Aaron, Beth, Luke, we've found her, she's OK, but we've taken her to Bournemouth Hospital for a check-up to make sure there's nothing untoward."

Beth screamed, Aaron running to her side, saying, "Oh my God Beth, they've found her, where was she, is she hurt, is she asking for us? Where did you say she was?"

April repeating what she'd said, knowing it probably didn't get through the first time. Luke was jumping all over the place, cheering and crying at the same time. He shouted, "I want to see Amanda now, can we go, Dad? I have to see that she's OK."

DC Bishop looked at all three of them, saying, "That's why we've brought two cars, we're taking you to her. Now look, I'm sure you have a thousand questions, but that can wait, let's just get you there."

Aaron was saying, "I'll ring my parents on the way and tell them what's happened, and we'll meet at the hospital, is she in A&E?"

"Yes, she's in a side room so she can't be disturbed, I'm told she's a bit shaken up, but that's to be expected, we'll find out when we get there," said April.

Aaron rang his father, who couldn't control his feelings and all you could hear down the phone were tears of joy. They set off to the hospital, knowing this was not going to be easy, but whatever it took to get Amanda back to how she was before this happened to her would be done.

They arrived at the hospital's A&E to find a sea of journalists rushing from their cars.

"How the hell do they know this has even happened?" asked Beth.

DC Bishop looked at them, saying, "Well, when we brought the suspects to the nick, there was some press there, they've been there for most of the time this has been going on, so my guess is they saw all this movement at the police station, put two and two together and realised that we may have found Amanda and where would you take someone who has been kidnapped? To the hospital to get her checked out. They're not daft, these press hounds."

They got out of the cars and April and Glen tried to put a safety barrier between them and the press. It sort of worked, but the shouting of questions from them made Luke annoyed. He shouted, "Why don't you leave us alone, we've come to see my sister, just leave us alone."

The family were shown where Amanda was, they looked through the window in the door, and could see she was fast asleep, she had a drip in her arm and a multitude of wires and probes all over her body. This was taking Beth back to when Amanda had had that tumour scare all those years ago.

They slowly walked in, trying not to wake her up and drew three chairs to the bedside. Aaron couldn't stop looking at her, his precious daughter was back with them, he couldn't ask for anything more, he got hold of Beth's hand and squeezed it tight, saying, "She's back, Beth, we got her back, I'm never going to lose sight of her again, that's a promise."

Beth said nothing, she nodded and asked if Luke was alright, he looked at them both, saying, "I'm with Dad, I want to make sure she is kept safe and that is what I'm going to do."

Both Aaron and Beth thought that was lovely and could see he meant it. There was a stirring in the bed as Amanda started to wake. At first, she had no idea where she was, and looked at the ceiling confusedly. She turned to look at who sat in the chairs and at first thought it was another one of her dreams.

Slowly, her parents came into view and she stared at them both, saying, "Mum, Dad, is that you? Where am I? How long have you been here?"

Beth got up and went to hold her hand but couldn't stop herself, she had to cuddle her and gave her the biggest hug she could. Amanda started crying, and held onto her mum for dear life, and said very quietly in her ear, "Mum, I'm so sorry, this shouldn't have happened, I was so stupid, I loved Matt with all my heart, but I knew I was being played, I just didn't do anything to stop it, I'm such a fool, Mum. They were there when those men took me. It's all coming back."

Beth pulled away from Amanda and looking into her eyes, said, "You're no fool, darling, when you're in love, you'll believe anything that is said to you, it's how it works, isn't it, Aaron?"

Aaron came right back, "It sure does. Love can make you blind, it happens all the time. But the good thing this time is that the people that did this to you have been arrested and will in the end pay for their stupidity, I'm sure of that."

All of a sudden, Amanda noticed that there was someone else to her left, she turned, saying, "Hello, bro. How you doing? I didn't see you there."

Luke smiled, and didn't say a thing, he got up and wrapped his arms around her neck, saying, "I'm so glad you're back, I can't believe I'm going to say this but I have missed you over the last few days. Has it been bad? They haven't hurt you, have they?"

Amanda went very quiet and started looking at the ceiling again. They all saw this and Aaron realised she didn't want to talk about it. Aaron said, "Right, I'm sure you are very tired, and us being here is great, and to see that you are safe and well is even better, but I think you need some sleep now Amanda, so were going to go home now. We have a lot of people to ring, tell them you are home and safe, so you put your head down and we'll see you later, OK?"

"No," said Amanda. "Don't leave me on my own."

"OK darling, I'll stay and keep you company, I'm sure Dad can sort the rest out, is that OK?"

"Yes, thanks. I don't think I want to wake up with no one next to me."

Luke jumped on her bed and put his arms round her neck, saying, "I'll never leave you on your own ever again. Never, I love you, Amanda."

Amanda smiled and put her arms around Luke, saying. "I love you too Luke, but I think we're going to have to have a conversation about when and where you can look after me, is that alright." She looked at her mum and they both began smiling at each other. Luke started laughing, then all the room was in laughter. Amanda thought to herself, *it's so good to be back.*

Beth stayed with Amanda while Luke went with Aaron to help him out, they said their goodbyes, and left.

Amanda watched them go and looked at her mum, she didn't have to say a thing, she pulled the bed clothes over her shoulders, closed her eyes and was asleep in minutes.

***

As Aaron and Luke made for the hospital exit, April, the liaison officer stopped them and asked if they would follow her into a room off the corridor, in there were Aaron's parents. Luke rushed up to Grandma Simpson and hugged her tight, saying, "Grandma, she's back, I've just seen her."

Grandma, with a smile on her face, replied, "That's brilliant, Luke."

Aaron came in. "Yeah, she looks a bit shaken up, but after what she's been through, who wouldn't? I know you want to see her but she was getting tired, so we left her to go to sleep. I think it was for the best, the nurse said she would ring us when she wakes and we can come back, it seems pointless us being there, she could sleep for hours. I'll ring you when they do, and we can all go at the same time, is that alright with you?"

Geoff and Mary looked a bit hurt, but understood what Aaron was saying and agreed to come back tomorrow, but insisted that if anything changed, they were to ring them. Aaron promised. April looked at all of them and said to Aaron, "We have a problem."

"What's that?" asked Aaron.

"The press, and now the TV have multiplied a bit, but don't worry, we have another exit that is round the back where there are no press and we can get you to safety."

Aaron looked at April, concerned, saying, "But what about Geoff and Mary, they're parked in the front, aren't you?"

Geoff smiled, saying, "Well, you see when we arrived, I saw the press outside, and thought it would be stupid to park right there in front of them, so I parked round the back. Clever, yes?"

Aaron laughed. "I now know where I get my intelligence from. Good move, Dad."

April came in again and suggested that they all leave by the exit at the rear, she had a car waiting to take them home and Geoff and Mary could go in their car to get home. They all agreed it was a great idea, and left the hospital.

Chapter 38

After spending nearly seven months questioning the suspects, getting all the evidence together and charging them with different offences, it was time to go to court.

The case was to start in March at Bournemouth Crown Court, but there was an objection from all the plaintiffs' barristers that it would be close to home and their clients would not get a fair trial and were making a request that the case be moved to Salisbury Crown Court.

This the judge denied and it started a week later. They were all tried at the same time, as the judge said they had all allegedly committed the same crime, so all could answer to that same crime. It was to last six weeks with all defendants pleading not guilty at first, but as evidence came out, especially from the different labs finding that the blood from the glass at the pharmacy was that of Matt Fisher.

The blood on the trainers found at the playground came back as Frank Bells and semen found on clothing belonging to Amanda was found to be Phil Turnbull's. The evidence made it impossible for the Boscombe Three to say they had nothing to do with the kidnapping.

DS Walters had found out that DS Hudson had known Mad Mick for over ten years, she had been feeding him intelligence about raids at all his factories and clubs over that period. She was really castigated by the judge who said it was bad enough to hear that a police officer, who is meant to serve the people of this community, should behave in this way and she should be ashamed of the fact that the wider world would think of her as evil.

When Maggie Taylor was called—she had been given immunity by the CPS for her help in catching the suspects—their pleas seemed to waver, and one by one, they changed their plea to guilty, except Phil Turnbull. He would plead not guilty to the rape.

It was obvious he didn't want a rape charge on his record, but the forensics were too strong for him not to be the rapist. He was leaving it to the jury. Because, for the most part, they'd all changed their plea, the trial was over in three weeks, and when the judge had finished summing up and sent the jury out, then it became a waiting game.

The jury were out three days and this had worried the prosecution. In their minds, it was too long, what was there to think about, it was an open and shut case, all the evidence pointed to them all. But, as they all said, you can never tell what a jury thinks.

In the barrister room, the door opened and the clerk of the court came in, telling them the jury had come to a decision. They all hurried to the courtroom and sat in their respective chairs and waited for the judge to appear and sit at his bench.

He called for the jury to be brought in, both defence and prosecution barristers were looking for any inclination or a sign that said guilty or not guilty, but there wasn't a one. They sat down, with the judge asking, "Will the foreman of the jury please stand?"

A woman nearest the judge, dressed quite smartly with a permed hairstyle looking to be in her sixties stood up.

The judge looked at her, asking, "Have you all come to a verdict that you all agree on?"

She replied, "Yes, Your Honour."

The judge said, "I would like you listen to the clerk of the court who will call the name of the accused and their crimes and I want you to tell the court if that person is guilty or not guilty, do you understand?"

"Yes, Your Honour."

"Will the defendants please stand up?"

The clerk of the court stood up. He was right in front of the judge's bench. He turned to his left and asked the jury foreman, "On the count of kidnapping, how do you find the defendant Matthew Fisher, guilty or not guilty?"

"Guilty," came the reply.

"On the count of drug dealing and drug trafficking, how do you find the defendant Matthew Fisher, guilty or not guilty?" asked the clerk.

"Guilty," came the reply.

"On the count of burglary, how do you find the defendant Matthew Fisher, guilty or not guilty?" Again, asked the clerk.

"Guilty," came the reply.

"On the count of kidnapping, how do you find the defendant Frank Bell, guilty or not guilty?" The clerk turned a page over.

"Guilty," came the reply.

"On the count of GBH on Amanda Simpson, how do you find the defendant Frank Bell, guilty or not guilty?"

"Guilty," came the reply.

"On the count of drug dealing, and possession with intent to supply, how do you find the defendant Frank Bell, guilty or not guilty?"

"Guilty," came the reply.

"On the count of kidnapping, how do you find the defendant Philip Turnbull, guilty or not guilty?"

"Guilty," was the reply.

"On the count of GBH on Amanda Simpson, how do you find the defendant Philip Turnbull, guilty or not guilty?"

"Guilty," was the reply.

"On the count of drug dealing and possession with intent to supply, how do you find the defendant Philip Turnbull?"

"Guilty," was the reply.

"And on the rape of Amanda Simpson, how do you find the defendant Philip Turnbull?"

"Guilty," was the reply.

There was a noise coming from the defendants' box, Philip Turnbull was shouting, "I never did that, I wouldn't fucking rape anybody. You've got that wrong. When I get out, I'll come for all of you."

While Turnbull was screaming away, the judge was banging his gavel on the bench shouting, "Order! Order!" and requesting that Turnbull be removed from his court, which he was, but not without him being tasered and handcuffed both on his hands and feet. The noise was abated and the judge told the clerk to carry on.

"On the count of kidnapping, how do you find the defendant, Sally Hudson, guilty or not guilty?"

"Guilty," came the reply.

"On the count of bringing the police force into disrepute, how do you find the defendant Sally Hudson?"

"Guilty."

"On the count of kidnapping, how do you find the defendant Michael Drake? Guilty or not guilty?"

"Guilty," was the reply.

"On the count of running a drugs cartel from a premises in Boscombe, how do you find the defendant Michael Drake, guilty or not guilty?"

"Guilty," was the reply.

The judge thanked the jury for all their good work and diligence on what was a very harrowing case, and they were free to go. He told the accused that sentencing would be immediate.

He started with Hudson, saying, he was sentencing her to the maximum he was allowed in this case and that was 18 years in jail. There were sentences for Frank Bell for kidnapping, GBH, drug dealing, possession with intent to supply, for which he got 22 years.

Phil Turnbull was convicted of kidnapping, GBH, rape, drug dealing, possession with intent to supply for which he got 27 years. The judge commented that to commit the evil act of rape is the evillest crime anyone can commit on another human being and had taken that into consideration in his sentencing.

Matt Fisher was convicted of kidnapping, burglary, drug dealing, possession with intent to supply and got 20 years. The judge then came to Michel Drake, informally known as Mad Mick.

"Mr Drake, where do I start with you?" he said. "You have terrorised the south of England for over ten years, you have had people tortured, we have found out that people have disappeared; we know that this is not your first kidnapping, and that the rise in crime and drugs use in the south is all down to your cartel."

"With all that said, I have no problem sentencing you to life in prison, with a maximum of 35 years before you are eligible for parole." The judge then addressed the court, "In front of you are the lowest of all human beings, a bunch of drug dealers, who were kidnappers, rapists, murderers and in the mix, only way to put it, is a bent cop."

"It has not been my pleasure to officiate over this case, but it has been a great pleasure to send you all down for a long time. Let this be a lesson for all out there. Crime doesn't pay."

Epilogue

Aaron and Beth, and of course, Luke, were inconsolable when they were reunited with Amanda and there were lots of hugs and kisses all around. The whole family were offered therapy and they all took it, Amanda doing especially well as they found out that she had been raped in her ordeal.

Amanda told her mum, and Beth was a pillar of strength for her daughter. It was hard for Beth but they talked all the time about both of their ordeals, touching on anything that came up, even the rape. Beth thought that their whole lives had come full circle, and she felt so bonded to Amanda and couldn't wait to have more of these bonding moments. Because their Amanda was back.

The End

Printed in Great Britain
by Amazon

47219738R00099